THE
UNDEADLIEST
QUEST

Jesse Stimpson

The Undeadliest Quest

First edition Hardcover November 1ˢᵗ 2023

First edition Paperback November 1ˢᵗ 2023

To my amazing, crazy family.

I love you all and couldn't have done any of

This without you. And especially thanks to my

Parents. Again, so sorry I forgot to add a

Dedication page to my first book, but you're

The ones who gave me ADHD, so it's really

Your fault.

Chapter 1: The Question

If someone had told Gabe how his story was going to end, he never would've joined his best friend on his dangerous quest.

It all started when they were in fifth-period math class. Gabe was sitting next to Charlie, who was pulling the fake textbook maneuver. You know, the one where you put a small book inside the pages of a large textbook, so the teacher thinks you're paying attention, but you're actually reading something fun. Charlie pulled this maneuver a lot, meaning Gabe had to take all the notes for him to copy later.

Something he did because Charlie was his best friend, and best friends sometimes did things for each other they didn't want to do. Like the time Charlie defended him against the bully who called him *taco boy*. The bully had been six inches taller than Charlie, but he wouldn't let anyone call Gabe rude names.

Just like Gabe wouldn't let Charlie fail 7th-grade math. He checked the whiteboard and scribbled the rest of the equation before Ms. Jadyson could erase it. He was almost finished when Charlie hit his side.

"Hey, Gabe?" he whispered. Gabe shushed him. He was having a good day and didn't want to ruin it by being sent to detention for talking during class.

Charlie didn't care. He leaned closer to Gabe and whispered, "I have an important question to ask you later."

Okay, that got Gabe's attention. It also made him nervous. Charlie probably had some dumb idea that was going to get them both in trouble.

"Whatever it is, no," Gabe said.

Their teacher turned and gave them a stern look. Charlie and Gabe sat up straight in their seats and pretended to pay attention until Ms. Jadyson turned back to the board.

Charlie leaned over again. "You don't even know what I'm going to ask you."

"Stop talking," Gabe whispered. He pushed Charlie away and tried to give his attention to the next equation. It was not easy. Charlie kept staring at him, wiggling his eyebrows.

Gabe ground his teeth. He loved his best friend, but sometimes he could drive him crazy.

Charlie put his textbook down, pulled his notebook out of his backpack, and started scribbling. He ripped the page out of his notebook, folded it into a square, and slid it to Gabe.

Gabe slid it back.

Charlie slid it back again.

Gabe grabbed the note and shoved it in his pocket. He didn't care what it said. He wanted to finish the last five minutes of class without getting in trouble. Charlie could hold off for just five more minutes.

Charlie scribbled on another sheet of paper, tore it out, and again folded it and slid it to Gabe.

Gabe groaned, making everyone in the room turn to stare at him. He slapped his hand over his mouth, dying of embarrassment.

Ms. Jadyson's eyes went to the note between the two boys. She frowned as she walked over to the table, her high heels clacking with every slow step, and picked up the folded paper.

She turned to Gabe, shook her head, and said, "Honestly, I expected more from you. Since this is rare, I'll give you one warning, but if I see you passing notes again, I'll have to give you both detention." She turned to Charlie. "Understood?"

They nodded.

She turned back to the whiteboard. Gabe stared daggers at Charlie until the bell began to ring.

Gabe shoved his books in his bag and headed towards the hallway. Luckily, Charlie wasn't in either of his last two classes, so there was no chance he could get him into trouble.

Well, maybe a little chance. Charlie could get anyone in trouble.

"Gabe!" Charlie shouted.

Gabe pushed himself through the group of middle schoolers, hoping to get lost in the crowd.

Charlie's shouts were drowned out by the other students trying to have quick conversations between classes.

Gabe got to his next class, English, three minutes before the bell rang. He sat in his usual seat and tapped his fingers on the desk.

That's when he remembered the note in his pocket.

He tried not to think about it. Whatever was written was probably something that was going to get him in trouble, and if he got in trouble, he would get detention. If he got detention, he would have to miss baseball practice. If he missed baseball practice, he would have to explain to his parents why he missed baseball practice, and that would lead to them finding out he'd gotten in trouble—which was why he couldn't read the note.

He glanced at the clock. Twenty-seven seconds had passed since he'd sat down. Two minutes and thirty-three seconds were left until his class started, then he would be distracted and wouldn't think about the note.

Another twelve seconds went by before he'd had enough.

There was no way a note could get him in trouble. He could read the note, and when he knew what his ridiculous friend wanted to ask him, he would be able to relax.

He slipped the note out of his khakis and unfolded it. Written, in terrible handwriting, were the words:

'I'll tell you after school. Can't risk this note getting in the wrong hands. Be prepared.'

Gabe sighed and rested his head on the desk. Great.

A thousand thoughts ran through his mind as his English teacher explained their essay assignment.

Maybe he wanted to ask if Gabe would come with him to his gymnastics tournament that weekend? Charlie never talked about Gymnastics at school because kids made fun of him for it.

But that wouldn't be something he needed to be prepared for. He'd been to many of Charlie's tournaments.

Gabe's stomach turned. Maybe Charlie was sick. Maybe he needed a kidney or part of Gabe's liver.

No, that didn't make sense either. Of course Gabe would give Charlie his kidney, but he didn't look sick enough to need a new one.

By the end of English class, he had gone through every possible question Charlie could ask, but none made sense. He would have to wait until they got to the buses.

After Science, he ran to the bus he and Charlie took to the community center. Charlie was already on, sitting in their usual seat in the middle row.

He was still reading the book from Math class. He was almost done, meaning he'd read it through his last two classes. Gabe had no idea how Charlie was passing any class where he wasn't right next to him, taking notes for them.

Gabe shoved himself in their seat and said, "Okay, now that school's over, ask me. Ask me the big, important, no one can know, question."

Charlie glanced around. There were at least thirty other kids on the bus.

"Not here. Later. After practice."

Gabe wanted to punch the seat in front of him. He was so frustrated Charlie wouldn't just ask him, but he couldn't force his friend to speak, so he crossed his arms and sat in silence for the hour-long bus ride.

When they got to the community center, they went their separate ways. Charlie walked a few blocks to his gymnastics studio while Gabe went behind the center for baseball.

Gabe was not good at baseball. Scratch that—he was horrible! But his father was excellent at it, so he signed Gabe up every spring and fall, hoping the boy would get better with practice.

He never did.

This practice was even worse because his mind was on what Charlie wanted to ask him. He didn't even swing at the ball when the coach pitched to him, and he got hit in the knee when he was supposed to be guarding second base.

"Have a good evening, Gabe!" his coach shouted as Gabe limped away. He didn't seem to notice Gabe was distracted all practice, which showed just how bad he usually performed.

He walked a few blocks, ignoring the growing pain in his swollen knee. He got to the gymnastics center as Charlie was walking out backward, waving to his group.

"Bye, Jase. Bye, Tamika. Bye, La-Hey!" Charlie shouted as Gabe pulled him away from the door. "That was rude."

Gabe dragged Charlie until they were many feet away from the building and anyone who could listen.

"Okay, ask me. What is so big that you've made me wait all afternoon?" Gabe asked, his fingers tapping his leg.

Charlie shook his head. "Not here. At my house."

Gabe stood firm. "No. Here. Now. Ask me."

Charlie turned down the sidewalk and kept walking to his house like he knew Gabe would follow.

He did.

Finally, after another seventeen agonizing minutes, they arrived at Charlie's house.

Charlie wanted to stop by the kitchen first for a snack, but Gabe couldn't wait a moment longer. He was about to pee himself.

He grabbed Charlie's hand and dragged him up the stairs. He pushed Charlie into his room and shut the door behind them.

Charlie ran over to his blinds and closed them as though they were being watched by the F.B.I. and their lips could be read.

Charlie opened his desk drawer. "Duct tape, duct tape. Where did I put the duct tape?"

Gabe shoved Charlie onto his bed.

"ASK ME NOW!" Gabe screamed in an octave he'd never used before.

Charlie grinned.

"Okay, but if I tell you, you have to promise not to tell anyone else, okay?"

Gabe nodded so fast his neck hurt.

"In order to ask you this question, you need to know something first." Charlie placed his hands on Gabe's shoulders and looked him dead in the eye. "I come from a family of vampires." ☐

Chapter 2: The Explanation

Gabe had obviously just misheard Charlie.

He couldn't have possibly said what he thought he'd said. His friend wasn't the best at paying attention in school, but he was still smart. He knew vampires didn't exist. Maybe Gabe's ears were broken.

"What?" Gabe asked.

"My great-great-grandmother was a vampire."

Okay, so Gabe's ears were working. It was Charlie's brain that was broken.

"Charlie," Gabe said slowly, "you do know that vampires aren't real, right?"

Gabe didn't want to make him upset, but they were in middle school. Kids got beat up for still believing in mermaids and werewolves and such.

Charlie shook his head. "Oh, sweet, naive Gabe. Come here." Charlie made his way across his room, but Gabe decided not to follow. He had no idea what lurked on his friend's floor since it was always covered in a layer of dirty clothing. If his room ever looked like that, he would've been grounded faster than his papa could shout, "Sin videojuegos!" His dad always spoke in Spanish when he was upset.

He watched as Charlie pulled open his bottom dresser drawer, which was filled with crumpled-up clothing. Charlie threw all the scarves, socks, and pairs of hopefully clean underwear behind him until the drawer was empty.

"Uh, Charlie," Gabe asked as he tip-toed across the room as though avoiding a group of landmines. "How is an empty drawer going to prove the existence of— Woah!"

Charlie slid his finger along the back of the drawer and popped a false bottom out. Underneath was a pile of spread-out photos, some in black and white, others in color. Charlie scooped the pictures up and carried them to the middle of his room. He kicked the clothing out of the way and made a clear spot on the floor then dumped the photos onto it.

He spread his hands across the photos to scatter them out then said, "See?"

Gabe sat across from him and checked out the images. The black and white ones looked like they were taken a hundred years before. The women were wearing flowing, thick dresses that covered their shins, and the men were all dressed in button-up shirts and ironed pants.

The photos in color were taken over multiple decades. Some were so worn, they had tears and stains. The others looked freshly printed. Gabe loved looking at the photos as he was interested in both history and photography, but he didn't know how they had anything to do with their conversation.

"I don't see any sharp teeth or mugs filled with blood. How does a bunch of old photos prove the existence of vampires?" Gabe asked.

Charlie slapped his forehead. "Look at them closely. Doesn't something seem off?"

Gabe looked over the photos again, but they seemed normal to him. Some of the ones in color resembled photos his papa had shown him from back when he was a young boy.

But then he noticed something strange. The people in the black and white photos were the same people in the colored photos, and they were the same age in all of them. They had the same hair though styled in different ways to reflect the decade they were taken. They even had the same freckles.

But there was a logical, non-magical reason for that, right?

"These are probably edited. My mama and papa have a photo of them that makes it look like they were in the wild west. They got it on their honeymoon to Hawaii."

Charlie deflated like a balloon. His smile turned to a frown, and he groaned. "Come on, Gabe. I'm telling the truth."

Gabe wanted to believe, but he couldn't. Someone in Charlie's family must've played some rude prank on him, and now he had to clean up the mess.

"I believe," Gabe started, making Charlie's smile start to return, "that you believe." Charlie frowned again.

"Fine, uh…" Charlie wrung his hands as he stared at the photos. "Oh, I got it." He ran his fingers along the pictures, picking out a few, then laid them in a line.

He pointed to the first photo in the line and said, "Look at this baby. Look at who's holding it."

In the black and white photo was a young woman holding a small baby, dressed in a white, flowing dress, in front of a church.

"Now look at this." Charlie pointed to the next black and white photo. In this one, the same woman was standing next to a five-year-old boy, wearing suspenders. She had her arm wrapped around him in a motherly way.

Gabe looked at the next photo, then the next, then finally the last. In each photo the boy was a few years older. First, he was ten, then a teenager, and finally an adult, but the woman stayed the same. She even looked younger than the boy in the last photo.

Gabe looked back and forth, from the second photo of the five-year-old boy to the last photo of the grown man. They had the same hair, the same mole on their chin, even the same folded left ear. They had to be the same person.

Gabe shook his head and pushed himself away until his back met the bedroom door. It couldn't be true. There had to be some sort of explanation. Maybe the man in the last photo was the father of the boy in the first photo. But then, why would the father's photos be in color when the son's photos were in black and white?

Maybe... maybe his friend was telling the truth?

Gabe shook his head. "No, this isn't possible. How would that even work? How would drinking other people's blood keep you from aging? From dying?"

Charlie shrugged. "Magic?"

Gabe's stomach started to hurt as his chest grew heavy. "Magic is real too?"

What wasn't real? Next Charlie was going to tell him zombies and Bigfoot exist.

"Obviously. My great-grandpa even taught me a spell. Wanna see it?"

Gabe wanted to go home and curl up in his bed with a fluffy blanket, but he had to see. He needed proof that magic was real. "Okay," he whispered.

Charlie locked his door. "Don't want my parents walking in. They hate everything to do with magic."

That didn't surprise Gabe. Charlie's parents hated everything to do with fun. While Gabe's parents were strict with chores and homework, they also watched movies together, made s'mores, and sometimes even traveled when his mama was feeling good.

Charlie's parents were the opposite. They let him keep his room a mess and never checked his report cards, but they didn't do anything together either. Sometimes they would leave for vacations without him, but Charlie never minded since they left him at Gabe's.

Charlie reached under his bed and pulled out a small, wooden box with a strange carving on the top as though someone had taken a knife and twirled it around, making spirals that resembled flowers.

"Aperta," Charlie whispered to the box. The carvings lit up, and the box clicked open. Charlie raised his brows at Gabe, but he still wasn't convinced. There were plenty of voice-activated password locks.

Charlie opened the box. Gabe peaked over his shoulder, not knowing what to expect.

He tilted his head when he noticed the only thing in the box was a pile of small leaves.

"Seriously?" Gabe asked. Charlie ignored him as he took one of the tiny, green leaves and laid it in the palm of his hand, placing the box beside them.

Charlie twirled his pointer finger on top of the leaf while whispering, "Oriri." The leaf spun on his palm before lifting into the air. It twirled faster and faster until it looked like the blades of a helicopter.

"Woah" was all Gabe could think to say as the leaf turned so fast, it created a small gust of wind. Once it gathered enough speed to barely be seen, Charlie snapped, and the leaf burst into a tiny fireworks show.

Gabe jumped back, his heart racing. He pulled his knees to his chest and rested his nose against them.

This was the craziest thing he'd ever learned, even crazier than learning caterpillars melt in their cocoons to turn into butterflies. Even weirder than learning his best friend only changed his underwear every five days—a fact he often tried to forget.

If magic was real, it meant everything he thought he knew, everything his parents and teachers had taught him about the world, was wrong. That his friend knew more about the world than people who had spent their entire lives studying it. Gabe didn't know how to process this information. He didn't know if he even wanted to. If he believed in a world with magic, a world with vampires, that meant he had a new world of things to fear. Would he be able to sleep at night, knowing there are things that go around, drinking people's blood? That there are things that would hurt others, to keep themselves alive?

"Wait," Gabe said, remembering how to speak. "If vampires are real, and your grandmother—"

"Great-great-grandmother."

"Yeah, if your great-great-grandmother was one, does that mean she went around attacking people?"

Charlie shook his head. "No, never. My great-great-grandmother was one of the sweetest people ever. She drank from blood bags. She told me there were good vampires and bad vampires, just like people."

Yeah, but bad people were a lot easier to stop than bad vampires, who had super strength and speed. Gabe's head started to hurt as though learning all this new information was causing his brain to expand enough to make his skull crack. He didn't want to talk about vampires anymore. He wanted to forget about them.

His stomach growled, making him sigh in relief.

"I gotta go. My mama's making lasagna, and it's probably almost ready." He jumped to his feet and turned to open the door, but just as he reached for the handle, Charlie grabbed his arm to stop him.

"Wait, I wanted to ask you something, remember?"

Uh, oh. Gabe did not like the sound of that.

"If this involves becoming vampire hunters, I would like to remind you that we are both less than five feet tall, and I never passed the ten-push-up test in Gym."

Charlie laughed. "No, that's dumb and dangerous. No, my plan is way, way cooler." He clasped his hands together and smiled a mischievous grin. "No, I don't want to hunt any creatures. I want to become a creature, and I want to know if you do too."

Gabe had a bad feeling he knew what his friend was saying, but he played dumb.

"What do you mean?"

Charlie took a step closer, placed his hands on Gabe's shoulders, and said, "I mean, I want to get turned into a vampire, and I want you to join me. Come on, Gabe. Wanna become a vampire?"

Chapter 3: The Decision

Gabe pulled at the collar of his jacket as he ran for his bike lying in Charlie's front yard, the place he'd left it that morning. He hopped on the bike and rode down the street, to his house at the bottom of the hill. The ride up to Charlie's was a struggle, but the ride back down was glorious. The wind flowed through his curly hair, pushing against his face so fast it became numb. It was magical.

Gabe gulped. He didn't want to think about anything magical. Magic used to be fun. It was supposed to be books about wizards saving the world or using powers for fun things like making cheetahs dance. It was supposed to be funny.

It was supposed to be fake.

Now that he knew it was real, he didn't find it fun. After Charlie asked him to become a vampire with him, he stood frozen for a moment. How could you respond to your friend asking such an outrageous question?

Gabe told him he need a day to think about it, but that was a lie. There was no way he was going to turn into some scary, blood-drinking, never dying monster. He just needed a day to think of a way to talk Charlie out of making a huge mistake.

He figured he could go home, write down all the reasons becoming a monster in middle school would turn out horribly, then Charlie would come to his senses, and they could go back to pretending they live in a safe, non-magical world.

Gabe skidded to a stop in his driveway. He jumped off his bike and guided it to the rack he'd built with his papa by their garage.

He entered through the garage, making sure to take his shoes off first. He was closing the door behind him when he heard a scream come from the kitchen.

"Mom!" he shouted as he made his way in.

His mother was sitting under the kitchen table with a fly swatter in her hand. Her face was blotched and covered with tears.

Gabe checked around the room, trying to see what had scared his mother, but there was nothing there.

Gabe sighed. This wasn't the first time he'd found his mother like this. See, Gabe's mother was sick. She didn't have cancer or diabetes. She didn't have something temporary, like the flu. She was sick in her brain. She had something called Schizophrenia. It makes her see things that aren't really there. Sometimes she gets scared when she sees something, so she hides.

Gabe crouched under the table but didn't get too close. His father always told him to keep a little bit away from his mother if she was ever upset because her brain might trick her into thinking he was scary too.

"Mom, it's okay. You're safe."

Gabe's mother shook her head. She squeezed the fly swatter tighter.

"They're gonna hurt me. Don't look into their eyes," she whispered as she squeezed her eyes shut.

Gabe bit his lip as he held back the tears that always threatened to spill when his mother was scared. He never let them fall. He had to be strong when she couldn't.

"Mom, there are no bad guys. Look at me. It's Gabe. I'm here, and I'll keep you safe."

She turned to look at him. At first, she didn't seem to recognize who he was, but then she put the fly swatter down and took his hand. He guided her out from under the table and helped her sit in a chair.

"Are you okay?" Gabe asked. His mother nodded. "Do you want some water?"

She nodded again, but before he could turn away, she grabbed his arm and whispered, "I'm sorry."

Gabe shook his head. "It's okay." It wasn't her fault.

He walked over to the cabinet, but as he reached for a glass, the microwave timer started beeping. Gabe ran to turn it off, but it was too late.

His mother jumped from her seat with wide eyes. "They're coming for me," she said. She ran for the door.

"Mom, no!" Gabe shouted as he ran after her. He grabbed for her arm, but she pulled away and ran to the front yard. He watched as she kept going, into the darkness of night.

"Mama!" he shouted from his front porch. He wanted to go after her, but he knew it was safer to call his papa. He would know what to do.

He ran back inside and grabbed his mother's cellphone from the table. After telling his father what had happened and hearing a few Spanish curse words, his father told him to stay put. He promised Gabe his mother would be okay.

Gabe trusted his father, so he stayed home. He grabbed the slightly burnt lasagna out of the oven then sat and waited for his parents to return. He didn't touch the dish even though he knew his mother would've wanted him to eat. He couldn't imagine putting anything in his stomach. It felt like it was tied up in a hundred knots.

He sat alone at his kitchen table for an hour. He then realized he should put the lasagna away before it went bad, so he covered it in plastic wrap and placed it in the fridge, ignoring the hunger growls.

He went to the living room and sat on the couch, staring at the TV but not turning it on. He wouldn't have been able to pay attention to it.

His eyes started to droop. He checked the clock. 10:47. It was over an hour past the time he was usually in bed. He turned to look at his bedroom door, but it sat at the end of a long, dark hallway.

He hadn't feared the dark since he was five. Any other night he would walk down the hall and sit on his bed, possibly crack open a book if he wasn't too tired.

But that was before he learned about the existence of vampires. That was before his world changed forever. Even if he could convince Charlie to not become a vampire, he still knew they were out there. There could be one right outside his windows.

He jumped to his feet and made sure every window and door was locked before shutting the blinds. He went back to the couch and sat up straight, staring back at the blank TV, praying his father would get home soon.

When he was little, he was scared a green monster would come into his room and eat him. His mama would laugh and say it was the monster in his stomach telling him he was hungry. She would bring him some crackers and sing him to sleep.

He would give anything to go back to those nights, back when the world was safe, and his mama could protect him from anything.

He was just about to lay his head back on the couch when the front door swung open. Gabe turned around and frowned when he saw only his Papa walk through the door.

He had dark circles around his eyes and bags underneath. His stomach was growling, and he was rubbing his back, something he always did after a long day.

Gabe stood from the couch to give his father room to sit.

"Where's mama?" he asked.

His papa sighed and reached out for Gabe's hand. "Come, sit here."

His papa took off his red baseball cap and ran his fingers through his balding hair.

"Your Mama was running across the street when a car hit her. She's going to be okay," he added when Gabe stared to hyperventilate. "But she broke her leg. They're going to keep her in the hospital for a few days."

Gabe didn't hold back the tears this time. He let them fall free, making his cheeks and sweatshirt wet.

"It's all my fault," Gabe said.

His papa wrapped his arms around him and shook his head.

"No, my hijo, none of this was your fault. You did exactly what you were supposed to do. You called me and your mama's gonna get better. She has a doctor helping heal her leg and her brain, okay?"

Gabe nodded, but pulled away. He didn't deserve his father's support. He couldn't keep his own mother safe. He deserved to be alone and think about what he'd done. "I'm going to go to bed now."

His papa patted his shoulder, and Gabe stood and walked to his room. Now that his father was home, he felt a little safer. His papa was so strong, he might be able to take on a vampire. At least a small one.

Besides, Gabe didn't feel he deserved to be protected. He couldn't keep his mom safe. He wasn't strong enough to stop her from leaving or fast enough to stay by her side. Maybe if he was next to her, he could've pushed her out of the car's way, and she would be home.

He kicked his cleats off by his bed then slipped under the covers, still wearing his baseball uniform. He didn't deserve to be comfortable.

He needed to be bigger, needed to be grown up, so he could help his mama, but it wasn't like he could grow any faster.

Gabe sat up, his eyes wide with an idea. He tossed the covers to the side and opened his bedroom window. Thankfully, he was on the first floor. He threw his legs out then leaned his head underneath the top and jumped to the ground. His socks became soggy in the wet grass.

He ran to his bike but then realized how dark it was outside. It would've been bad if he got into a car accident the same night as his mother. He placed the bike onto his homemade rack and walked along the edges of his neighbor's yards, guided by the light of the moon.

He got to the top of the hill where Charlie's house sat. He ran around to the back and tried to figure out a way to get Charlie's attention.

"Charlie!" he whisper-shouted, hopefully loud enough to wake Charlie but not his parents. They would send him home, and his papa would not be happy about him sneaking out, especially after the night they had.

Gabe looked around the backyard for something small enough to throw at the window without breaking it but big enough to cause a sound. He ran to Charlie's mother's garden and grabbed a few mulch chips.

He put all his strength into his first throw, but it wasn't high enough to reach Charlie's second-story window. He threw a bigger piece, hoping all the baseball practice had paid off, but instead of hitting the window, it hit the drainpipe, bounced off, and whacked him in the eye.

"Ow!" he screamed then covered his mouth.

"Gabe?" Charlie asked with his head sticking out the window. "What are you doing here?"

Gabe's toes wiggled in the wet grass as he tried to gather the courage to say what he wanted to say.

"We need to talk. I've made up my mind."

Charlie grinned and pulled his head away from the window. Gabe assumed he'd gone to unlock the back door for him. Instead, Charlie stuck his head back out the window a moment later with a rope ladder in his hands.

"My parents bought this for me in case of an emergency, and I think this is an urgent conversation."

He tossed the ladder out the window and connected the top to the frame.

"Come on," he said, waving Gabe up.

Gabe tugged at the ladder a few times. He wanted to make sure it wouldn't collapse when he was halfway up, causing him to fall and break his back before they even started their dangerous mission. Once he was confident the latter would not fall, he placed his foot on the bottom step and slowly climbed up. As soon as his fingers touched the window frame, he pulled himself up and threw himself into the room.

"Ow!" he said for the second time in a matter of minutes as he rubbed his shoulder. He'd forgotten Charlie had a hardwood floor since it was usually covered in clothes.

Wait a minute.

He glanced around the room with wide eyes because, for the first time ever, Charlie's room was spotless. There was no clothing on his floor, his desk was so organized you could do homework on it, his shoes were lined up by the door.

"It's clean," Gabe said, not believing his own eyes.

Charlie crossed his arms and grinned. "Yep, my parents were being super weird at dinner, like they thought I was hiding something. Which, I am, but they usually wouldn't pick up on something like that. Anyway, they were asking me a bunch of questions about what we were talking about up here, and I was like, baseball and stuff, but I think that made them more suspicious because I don't like baseball."

He was right. Gabe might not have been good at baseball, but at least he knew stats and positions. Charlie was never interested in any sports that included balls. His hobbies included gymnastics and fist fights behind the school because people made fun of him for being in gymnastics.

"I thought if I cleaned my room, they would be so shocked they'd forget I was acting suspicious," Charlie said.

"Charlie, wouldn't you cleaning your room make them more suspicious?"

Charlie froze. "Oh, no. Uh, quick, help."

He ran to his desk and knocked over a cup of pencils then pulled all the clothes out of his drawers. He kicked them around until every inch of the floor was covered.

"Ah," Charlie said as he admired his work, "much better."

Gabe shook his head. He didn't have time for his friend's antics. He needed to get stronger and faster, and he needed to be those things now.

"Charlie, I made up my mind." Gabe took a deep breath, like his mother taught him to do when he was nervous. The thought of her made him want to cry, but he stayed strong. "I want to do it. I want to become a vampire with you."

Charlie shook his fist in the air. "Yes, awesome! I was hoping you'd say yes. I didn't think you would, Mr. Rules, but I hoped." He hit Gabe's shoulder. "We're gonna be awesome vampires. Hey, we can even fight bad vampires on the weekends."

Gabe placed his hand on Charlie's shoulder. "Let's not get ahead of ourselves."

Charlie shrugged with a goofy smile. "Okay, so tomorrow we can go an—"

"No, not tomorrow. We must leave now."

He wanted to be a vampire by the time his mother got out of the hospital, and he didn't know how long it would take. He needed to be home to protect her from the monsters, both the ones inside her head and out.

"Right now? But it's dark outside, and I have a competition tomorrow."

Gabe grabbed Charlie's arms. "Please, Charlie. I want to do this with you, but I don't have a lot of time. Please, let's leave right now."

Charlie glanced at his window. "I don't know about this."

"Come on! We're about to become vampires. Don't tell me you're afraid of the dark."

Gabe knew he'd gotten under his friend's skin. Charlie liked to pretend he wasn't scared of anything.

Charlie walked to the side of his bed and grabbed a duffle from underneath. He threw it over his shoulder and said, "Okay, let's go."

Chapter 4: The Mythological Relative

They used the ladder to climb back out of Charlie's room. Once they reached the ground, Charlie dropped his duffel and dug through it till he found two flashlights.

"Be prepared for anything," he said as he handed one to Gabe.

They made their way around the house into the street before Gabe asked, "So, how does this work? We're not going looking for any like stray vampires, are we? You know good vampires who can turn us?"

Charlie shrugged. "I know a guy… kinda."

Gabe stopped walking and grabbed his friend's arm. "What do you mean *kinda*?"

Charlie pulled his arm away and gave him an apprehensive smile. "Well, you know how I showed you those pictures of my great-great-grandmother? Well, I knew her, but she died when I was little, but her brother is still alive. We even share the same name."

Gabe smiled, relieved. "Oh, so, you're close."

Charlie turned and started walking away. "No, the name thing was a coincidence. I've never actually met him."

Gabe slapped his arm.

"Hey!" Charlie shouted, rubbing his shoulder.

"You've never actually met him. You're taking me to a vampire you've never actually met."

Charlie waved his hands around making the light from his flashlight shine against the nearby houses. "No, but I know he's a good guy. My great-great-grandmother told me he was."

"But what if that's changed? What if he became evil because his sister died? What if he was the one who killed her?"

Charlie froze. He had not thought about that. "Well, then I guess we run." He flashed his flashlight in Gabe's face. "Listen, do you want to become a vampire or not? Because we can turn around and go home and think this through. I don't want to force you to do something life-changing if you don't want to."

Gabe stood up straight. "No, you're right. There's no safe way to become a vampire. This is our best option. Let's go."

They kept walking, and every so often Charlie would say another cool thing about becoming a vampire. "We wouldn't even need flashlights because we could see in the dark and our teachers would never give us homework because we can mind control them not to—"

"Whoa, whoa, whoa," said Gabe. "Vampires have mind control powers?"

Charlie stopped and tilted his head. "I don't know. They do in some movies. I hope they do."

Gabe hoped they didn't. It felt wrong forcing people to do and say and think things they didn't want to do, say, and think, like you were an evil dictator who didn't believe in free will.

Gabe frowned when, after walking for what might've been hours, they stopped in front of a regular, family home. He'd been expecting a cave or a mansion. This house was big, but it definitely wasn't a mansion. It was a normal two-story house in the middle of other, ordinary two-story houses. The front yard was freshly mowed. There was a truck out front and even plants by the driveway. It wasn't a place you'd expect a vampire to live.

"Charlie, are you sure we're in the right place?" Gabe asked.

Charlie nodded.

"Eighty-two percent sure, yeah."

He pulled out a crumpled piece of paper from his pocket. On it, written in scribbles, was something that resembled an address.

"Yeah. 2785 Lockcue Avenue."

Gabe check the address in the mailbox, which had the number 7258. "Charlie, either your address is wrong or we're at the wrong place."

Charlie was scratching the back of his neck, trying to remember if he'd written the numbers correctly when the lights on the front porch turned on.

"Hey!" a man shouted as the door swung open. "Who's out there?"

"I'm about to do something dumb. And I'm sorry," Charlie whispered before running to the house. "Charlie?" he shouted.

Gabe thought it was weird to hear his friend scream his own name, but he was too terrified about what might happen to think about it for long.

"Yeah. Who are you? And why are you shouting?" the older Charlie asked. It was a good question since young Charlie was standing at the bottom of the stairs, only a few feet away. "And what are you doing on my lawn?" The older Charlie placed his head in his hands. "I'm sorry. I sound like an old man." He chuckled.

Gabe took a few steps toward the two Charlies since older Charlie didn't seem like much of a threat. He looked to be about fifteen and couldn't be much over five feet tall. "Who are you? And what are you doing here at"—Older Charlie checked his watch—"one o'clock in the morning?"

Gabe had no idea it was that late. He felt bad for causing a disturbance, but Charlie didn't seem to because he asked, "Well, what are you doing up so late?"

Older Charlie crossed his arms. "Actually, I was asleep. But when you guys came into my yard, I was woken up by your 'not as quiet as you think' whispers."

Gabe's stomach started to churn. He was already regretting their decision. They were here to ask this man for a favor, and all Charlie had done was make him upset.

"Were we really that loud?" young Charlie asked. "Or was it your super hearing that helped you hear us?"

Older Charlie's eyes widened as he sputtered, "Uh, I don't know what you're talking about. It's late, and I'm sure your parents are worried about you."

"You're one to talk," young Charlie said. "What are you, fifteen?"

Older Charlie placed one hand on his hip and used the other to point his index finger at the boys. "I'll have you know that I am…" Older Charlie thought it over for a minute. "Thirty…" he said uncertainly.

"You've convinced me," younger Charlie said sarcastically.

Older Charlie glanced at the boys. "Listen, I don't know why you're here and I don't want to. Go home and—"

"I know you're a vampire," young Charlie said before older Charlie could close the door.

The older Charlie froze, turned around, and said, "Go home, kid. You don't want anything to do with this." Then he turned and shut the door.

That should have been the end of their adventure. When a vampire tells you to go home and not put yourself in danger, you should listen.

They did not.

Younger Charlie banged on the door until vampire Charlie swung it open. This time, his face was beet red. His shoulders sat next to his ears. "Listen, kids, I know you've been fed lies about vampires for years, but it's not all it's cracked up to be. It's dangerous and scary and people try to kill you."

Younger Charlie crossed his arms. "How long have you lived in this house?"

"About a decade, why?" older Charlie asked.

"So, you've lived in a safe neighborhood, in a nice house, for more than half our lives and you want to tell us your life is in danger. I don't believe it."

Older Charlie had had enough. He reached out and lifted younger Charlie by the collar, shoving him against the house.

"Listen, hear you little punk. I've lost people. I lost my best friend because of what we were."

"I know," young Charlie said calmly as though he wasn't being threatened by a vampire.

Older Charlie looked him up and down, confused. "What do you mean you know?" He pushed him harder against the wall.

"My name is Charlie, and I'm your great-great-great nephew." He held his hands out and shimmied them as though he was giving a dance performance.

Older Charlie lowered younger Charlie to the ground. "Oh," he said as he brushed young Charlie's shoulders. "Sorry, kid. I get a little nervous when people show up at my house in the middle of the night. You can understand."

Both boys nodded. Older Charlie cleared his throat and clapped his hands. "Well, why don't you come in and have some coffee?"

Gabe tilted his head. They've never been offered coffee before, being only thirteen, but they weren't going to tell this man that. They followed older Charlie into the house.

Gabe's gaze surveyed the living room. The ceiling rose twenty feet above their heads, but other than that, it looked like a normal family room. Messy, but a lived-in sort of messy.

There was a TV and a couch which was covered in unfolded blankets and jackets. There were many adult male jackets but also ones that looked like they belonged to a woman and a few others that belonged to a child around their age.

"Are you married?" Gabe asked as they checked out the photo frames filled with pictures of older Charlie and a woman who looked to be in her thirties.

Some of the pictures also had a boy in them. In the first picture, he was only a few years old, but in the others, he was much older.

"Yeah," he said as he held up his ring and smiled, "about seven years now."

"And you have a son? Vampires can have kids?" Charlie asked.

Older Charlie shook his head. "That's my wife's son, but I adopted him right after we were married. Vampires can't have kids, which is another reason why you shouldn't want to turn into one." Older Charlie grabbed a few mugs from the cabinet.

The boys stared at him.

"How did you know that was why we were here?" Gabe asked.

Charlie shrugged. "Why else would you be here? Let's see," he said as he filled the coffee pot with brown grounds. "You're here at one A.M., meaning this is probably a decision you made recently. That means you've given this little to no thought, which is not comforting."

Charlie continued to fiddle with the coffeemaker as Gabe squirmed in his seat. This was not going well. Younger Charlie didn't seem to notice as he stared in awe at his great-great-great-uncle.

Older Charlie pulled out a chair beside them and placed the coffee mugs in front of the boys.

"But I'm glad you're here," Older Charlie said. "I haven't seen a lot of Jo's family since she died, other than a few visits from her grandkids, which I'm guessing would be your grandparents." He laid back and rubbed his forehead. "Gosh, I'm old."

Young Charlie took a sip of coffee before saying, "Yeah, it's cool to meet you too. Most of my family is boring. It's awesome to know I'm distantly related to a vampire. Your life must be awesome."

Older Charlie smiled. "I have my good days."

Younger Charlie crossed his legs in his chair. "Tell me about them."

"Okay, well, one time—"

"Charlie," Gabe said, interrupting them and making both Charlies look and him questionably. "I mean, younger Charlie, you," he said, pointing to his best friend. "Gosh, this is going to be confusing."

Older Charlie waved at him. "Hey, it's fine. You can call me"—he bit the inside of his mouth— "Charles," he said as though he were saying a bad word.

"Great. Well, Charles, I'd like to hear your stories some other time, but right now, we're in a hurry. So, do you think you could turn us into vampires?"

Charles gripped his mug so tight his knuckles turned white. "Listen, kids. I'm sure you have many reasons why you want to become vampires, but I can tell you from experience, that's a really, really bad idea."

"Interesting, why?" Charlie asked.

"Well, there's the whole drinking blood thing. It's not very tasty."

Charlie shrugged. "My mom packs seaweed in my lunch for dessert. I can deal with un-tasty."

Charles squinted. "There's also the whole not growing up thing. You'd be a kid forever."

Charlie smiled.

"Exactly," said Charlie. "Not getting old. Always being young and fast and smart."

Older Charlie shook his head. That had not gone in the direction he had planned.

"Well, it doesn't matter because I'm not going to turn you, okay? And anyway, vampires can't even create other vampires. You'd have to have a witch turn you."

Charlie and Gabe turned to stare at each other with wide eyes.

Charles rubbed his thumb across the lip of his mug. "Something tells me I should have kept that info to myself."

"So, what you're saying is we need to find a witch?" Charlie asked as he leaned across the table. "Do you know any witches?"

"Yes, but I'm not going to tell you who or where to find her. It's not like she would turn two kids anyway," said Charles.

Charlie shrugged. "Then why not give us her address and let her tell us for herself."

"Because I don't need two kids bothering some witch. There are things they can do that give people nightmares." Charles shivered. "Anyway, since that conversation is over, I want you to know that you can stop by anytime. During the day," he added with a glare. "We have cookouts on Saturdays. Bring your families if you'd like. Well, bring your family," he said to Gabe. He pointed at Charlie and said, "I don't think your family likes vampires very much, which is another reason why this is a bad idea. Now, doesn't it feel better that we're past that?"

Charlie stood and waited for Gabe to do the same.

"Goodbye, Mr. Charles," Gabe said. "Thank you for your coffee."

Charles stood and asked, "Where are you going?"

"To find a witch since you won't tell us where yours lives."

Gabe didn't like the sound of that, but Charlie sounded confident. "You know, two kids in the woods looking for a which sounds kind of dangerous doesn't it, Gabe?"

Gabe's stomach was in so many knots, he didn't think he'd ever eat again, but he nodded. "Yeah, it does."

Charlie sighed. "Well, I guess if you're okay with two kids risking their lives. I wonder what you would think if your son was out there all alone, looking for someone who might kill him?" Charlie brushed his fingers along the picture frames.

Gabe had no idea his friend could be so manipulative. He was glad Charlie never used his powers on him. The boys were two steps from the door when Charles sped over with incredible speed, standing between them and their exit. His eyes were bright red, and his eyebrows were pointed down so sharply Gabe figured he could cut him with them.

"Or I could keep you here until your parents show up. Explain what you're doing and then make sure that they keep you locked up."

Gabe frowned. It sounded like a solid plan. He figured they were out of luck, but Charlie didn't back down. He took a step towards Charles.

"Sure, you could do that. We'd go home, be punished. Heck, they might even ground us until high school. They might put locks on our windows, might put alarms around our house, but there will be a moment, one day when they're not looking. Maybe we don't make it on our bus. Maybe we're playing outside one moment and then missing the next. We will keep trying over, and over until we get away again. We will search and search until we find a witch. Maybe she'll help us maybe she'll be our end. Who knows? But it will happen, and you can't stop it."

Charles's forehead was covered in sweat. He stared at Charlie, fear in his eyes. Why a grown vampire would fear a small teenager was beyond Gabe. Charlie shivered then said, "Okay, little demon child. I'll give you the address."

He stepped away from Charlie to the side table next to the couch. He picked up a little notepad and scribbled something onto it.

"Here," he said as he held it out to Gabe. "This is where you need to go. Ask for Eliah and say I sent you but also tell her I said this was a bad idea. When she tells you she won't turn you, will you please listen to her and stop this quest? At least until you're eighteen?"

That sounded fair, and besides, Gabe didn't want to hunt down other witches. He valued his life, but Charles didn't need to know that. Charlie held out his hand to Charles.

"Deal."

Chapter 5: The Witch Hunt

They walked an hour before finding a train station. The witch lived a few hours' drive from them, and neither owned a car nor could drive, so the bus it was.

The station was a small, brick building with a pergola off the side, covering where passengers would get on and off trains. Next to the pergola were two sets of tracks with a fence running between them.

The only person inside was a middle-aged woman, sitting behind a ticket counter. There were long, wooden benches on either side of the room, and above the lady's head was a board lit up with the trains schedules.

Charlie checked the board for a train leaving for Anian, North Carolina, the town the witch lived in.

"Here," Charlie said, pointing to a board. "There's a train that leaves in two hours that stops right outside Anian. How lucky are we?"

Gabe didn't feel lucky. He didn't know how he was supposed to make it two hours sitting around, thinking about the life-changing decision he was about to make.

Charlie didn't notice his anxiety and grabbed Gabe's arm before dragging him to the ticket line. It was empty, which wasn't surprising since it was two in the morning.

"Excuse me, ma'am," Charlie said to the ticket lady while flashing his innocent, lost boy smile. "My friend and I would like two tickets to the train leaving for Anian, North Carolina."

The woman looked the boys up and down with a scowl. Gabe didn't know if it was because she didn't like the idea of two kids out in the middle of the night or if it was Charlie's attire. He was still wearing his pajamas, which consisted of a hole-filled t-shirt and pants that were so short they sat above his ankles.

She typed something into her computer and said, "Alright, that'll be twenty-seven dollars."

Charlie frowned. He leaned over to Gabe and whispered, "Hey, you wouldn't happen to have twenty-seven dollars, would you?"

Gabe sighed. Nothing was going right, and they hadn't even made it to the witch yet.

"No." Gabe turned to the woman. "Excuse me, could we pay for the ticket some other way? Maybe we could mop the floors or organize some pamphlets or something?"

The woman shook her head. "Sorry, kids." She reached for the phone. "I could call your parents, and they could give you a ride to wherever you need to be."

"No!" Gabe shouted so loud; the woman dropped the phone. "I mean, no, ma'am. There's no reason for that. Have a great day."

He grabbed Charlie's arm and dragged him out of the train station. When they got outside, he pushed his back to the brick wall and closed his eyes.

"Great," he said. "We're never going to find the witch."

Everything was ruined. He wasn't going to be able to help his mom. He was going to be stuck as a defenseless kid for years.

He kicked his foot against the wall, grunted in pain then turned and opened his eyes. Charlie was sitting on the ground beside him, resting his head on one hand while he used the other to lift a leaf off the ground using magic.

That was it.

"Charlie, I have an idea," Gabe said. Charlie jumped to his feet, a smile growing on his face. "What if you can make money using magic?"

Charlie thought about it for a moment, unsure. "I mean, I probably could, but aren't there rules against using magic for personal gain?"

"Maybe in movies, but this is real life. There are no rules."

Charlie huffed.

"What?" Gabe asked.

"Nothing. It's, just, I didn't think I'd ever hear you say there are no rules."

He was right. Gabe was a big rule follower. It's not that he was a goody-two-shoes; there were just no rules he felt were worth breaking. Don't run down the hall kept him from tripping. No talking during class left the room quiet for learning. Making sure he got good grades would help him one day get into college.

But there were no rules to magic, as far as he knew. He'd found out it was real less than twelve hours before, so he wasn't an expert, but he didn't think there were magic policemen that would take them away in handcuffs for doing a little spell.

"Okay, I'll try." Charlie pointed to his hand and opened his mouth, but nothing came out.

"What's wrong?" Gabe asked.

"I realized I don't know a spell to make money appear. I only know the leaf one."

Gabe wanted to hit something. His arms felt tight as did his throat. There had to be a way to solve this problem. This couldn't be where their story ended.

"Think, Gabe, think... Uh, okay, when you were saying the spells, you were speaking in Latin, right?" Gabe asked. Charlie shrugged.

"I don't know."

Gabe sighed. "Of course not. Anyway, if you were speaking in Latin, then we would need to find the Latin word for money and then money would appear."

"Okay, what's the Latin word for money?" Charlie asked as though Gabe knew off the top of his head.

"Why would I know that? Latin is a dead language. No one speaks it except your great-grandfather apparently."

Gabe shook his head and started pacing. What were they going to do? They couldn't let a simple translation ruin their chances of making it to the witch. He placed his hands in his pockets, and that's when he realized he still had his mother's phone. He slid it out of his pocket, praying it had some battery left.

"Yes!" he shouted when the screen turned on. He typed the word money into a translation app. "Okay, try saying pecunia."

Charlie jumped and flailed his arms around, as though he were shaking out his nerves. He held up his palm, pointed to it, and said, "Pecunia."

A light shined from his finger, then in the palm of his hand, a gold coin appeared.

"It worked!" Charlie shouted as he held the coin high. Gabe wasn't as excited.

"Give me that," he said, taking the coin from Charlie to examine it. "We have a problem."

"What?" Charlie asked. "That is a perfect, gold coin, that I made from nothing, Gabe, nothing."

"Yes, but the problem is this is a freaking Aureus."

Charlie stared at him blankly. "I don't know what that is."

"It means we would be rich if we lived in ANCIENT ROME!" Gabe yelled then threw the coin on the ground.

Charlie grabbed the coin and stuck it in his pocket. "This doesn't make any sense. Why would I create a coin I didn't know existed?"

"Probably because you were speaking in Latin, and guess where Latin originated?" Gabe asked with a tense jaw.

"I have no idea, but by your reaction, I'm gonna guess Rome?" Charlie asked with a nervous smile.

Gabe shook his head. He didn't mean to get mad at Charlie; it wasn't his fault.

"I'm sorry. I'm just frustrated. Now we have no way of getting to Anian unless we want to walk and that will take forever."

Charlie raised his arms, making a w with his body. "At least once we become vampires, we'll have forever, and we won't have to worry about tired feet."

Gabe chuckled. He hadn't even thought about the other pros of being a vampire. Not getting worn out. Maybe he'd get better at baseball.

"Well, we'll never become vampires unless we can find a way to get Anian."

Charlie placed his hands on his hips and looked around, his eyes squeezed so tight, Gabe was surprised he could see out of them. He started to nod his head as though an idea was coming to him, but then he opened his mouth and said, "I have to go to the bathroom."

Gabe's head hit his chest.

They walked back into the train station and headed to the boy's bathroom. Gabe waited by the exit as Charlie used the restroom, humming the tune to a theme song. Gabe was about to figure out what TV show it was from when Charlie's hums stopped.

Charlie jumped out of the bathroom with wide eyes. "Gabe, I figured out how we can get to Anian."

Gabe took a step back. "Great, but can you wash your hands first before telling me?" He grew nervous, wondering what idea his friend could've come up with while using the toilet.

Charlie washed his hands, then they went back outside and sat on a bench by the entrance. Charlie crossed his legs and turned, so he was facing Gabe, his hands clenched into excited fists.

"Okay, so I was in the bathroom, and I realized, trains have bathrooms too." He smiled at Gabe as though that was a big realization for him.

"Good job. You realized people don't have to hold their pee for six hours at a time," Gabe said.

"Gabe, aren't you supposed to be the smart one? Anyway, bathrooms are for privacy. You can't go into the bathroom if someone else is in there. I'm sure that's illegal or something."

"Yes, very illegal, and wrong, but what does that have to do with any of this?" Gabe asked. He didn't know how much longer he could listen to his friend explain things he already knew.

"Oh, my gosh, Gabe, seriously? Think about it for a minute. If you're on a train when the ticket person comes by and you don't have a ticket, they will kick you off, but if you are in the bathroom, they can't force themselves in."

Maybe Charlie wasn't so dumb after all. But it couldn't be that easy, could it?

They waited on the bench till it was time to leave. In that time, they played backward I-Spy, where you have to name everything that's a certain color, except the thing the other person is thinking of. Then they played rock paper scissors and arm-wrestled, which Charlie won every time. He said it was from using the still rings in gymnastics.

Half an hour before the train left, people started arriving at the station. Couples, old people, young families, and anyone else you could think of hopped out of their cars and made their way into the station. Charlie and Gabe shoved themselves into the middle of the small crowd, trying to stay as inconspicuous as possible.

They found a family with a girl around their age. Gabe walked up to her and smiled. "I like your shoes," he said as he pointed to her Ninja Turtle high tops.

"Thank you," she said with a blush. "Michelangelo is my favorite. Who's yours?"

"Donatello." They continued to chat with the girl while the family made their way to the train. They figured if they could walk with people who had tickets they could get on and walk back to the bathroom to complete the second part of their plan.

Once the girl's family took their seats, Charlie grabbed Gabe's arm and dragged him to the bathroom.

It was tiny. There was only room for one person, as the toilet and sink almost touched. Charlie and Gabe stood shoulder to shoulder, their breathing heavy as they waited for the train to leave.

"I can't believe we're doing this," Gabe said while rubbing his churning stomach. "I've never broken a rule in my life."

"It's okay. When we get home, we'll volunteer at a charity or something to make up for it."

Gabe didn't think that was how it worked, but it was better than nothing. They shut their mouths and stayed quiet. After what felt like hours, but was only a few minutes, a loud huff came from the front of the train. The car shifted a bit, making Gabe's head hit the wall.

"Ow," he said, rubbing the pulsating spot on his forehead. Charlie held up his finger and shushed him.

They waited a while longer until they heard a man walking down the aisle, asking people for their tickets.

Every time he took a step closer to the bathroom, Gabe's heartbeat increased. He placed his hand on the wall for balance and closed his eyes, waiting for it to be over.

That's when they heard a knock at the door.

"Excuse me," the ticket man said. "I'm gonna need to take a look at your tickets, please."

The boys stayed silent. They stared at each other, neither knowing what to do. The man knocked again.

"Can you please answer me?" The man wiggled the doorknob.

Gabe bit his lip. Oh, this was not good. They were going to get in trouble, and their parents would be called and they would get dragged home and grounded forever. He couldn't risk it.

"Uh, no!" Gabe shouted. "Nina la arbol naraja las estrellas!" he said in a thick, Mexican accent, like his father's. He hit himself in the stomach and groaned. "Oh, no, no rojo ah luego."

The ticket man cleared his throat. "Oh, I'm sorry. I didn't mean to disturb you," he said then walked away.

Once they could hear his footsteps on the other side of the train car, they let out a deep breath.

"Dude," Charlie whispered, "I didn't know you could speak Spanish."

"I can't," said Gabe. "Those were a combination of all the words I know from my Abuela and *Dora the Explorer*. I was hoping he couldn't speak Spanish either."

"Well, that was quick thinking." They sat on the floor, facing one another, and gave each other a fist bump.

"Now we just have to ride in here for five hours. At least it's not smelly," Charlie said.

Gabe rested his head against the door and closed his eyes. He hadn't realized how tired he was until he was able to rest. He drifted to sleep.

Chapter 6: The Hidden World

As Gabe slept, *he dreamt of his mother. She was lying on the ground, one arm splayed over her face, the other resting beside her.*

"Mom," Gabe yelled, running towards her. She barely moved as he kneeled beside her.

"The monsters," she said as she peeled her arm away from her face. "They got me." She grabbed his shirt and stared at him with glowing black eyes. "You let them get to me. Why did you not save me?"

Gabe shook his head. He was too late. He couldn't save his mother. "No, I'm sorry. I tried. I promise."

She shook him. "It's too late."

"No, no!" he screamed.

"Wake up, dude!" she shouted back.

"What?" he asked before his mother disappeared and he was back in the train bathroom, face to face with a nervous Charlie.

"Dude," Charlie asked, "are you alright?"

He wasn't, but he nodded. It was a dream. He still had time.

"Are we there yet?"

"Yep." Charlie stood and held his hand out. "We gotta hurry before they notice us."

They slipped out of the bathroom and into the crowd of exiting riders. As they got off, they passed a sign that said, 'Welcome to Anian, home of the world's biggest, sweet potato fries.' They headed over to where people were entering and exiting the train station.

"Okay, we need to get to…" Charlie pulled the crumbled address out of his pocket. "Farmers Fresh Meadows."

"How exactly are we supposed to find Farmers Fresh Meadows?" Gabe asked.

Charlie shrugged. "We ask."

They went into the station, which resembled the one they left, except this one was much brighter thanks to the large windows that brought in plenty of natural light. There were only a few people in the ticket line, so they waited until it was their turn.

Charlie asked the ticket man, "Excuse me, sir, could you tell us where Farmers Fresh Meadows is and how to get there?"

The man smiled and crooked his head to the side. "Why would you want to go there? That's private property. No one is allowed to go around there."

Oh, great, not only did they want to disturb a witch, but they'd be trespassing as well. Gabe might as well throw himself in jail for all he's done.

"Right," Charlie said. "But our, uh, grandmother lives near there, and we were visiting her."

The man's smile grew as he tilted his head even more. "Why would you wanna go there? That's private property. No one is allowed to go around there."

The boys turned to each other. "Yeah," said Charlie. "You just said that, but I would like to visit my grandma, so…"

The man tilted his head so far to the right, they thought it might roll-off. "Why would you wanna go there? That's pri—"

"Yeah, yeah, private property. We get it." Charlie waved the man off and pulled Gabe out of line. The man's head returned to its normal, upright position, and he started selling tickets to the person behind them as if nothing happened.

"Okay, that was weird, right?" Gabe asked.

"Yeah, but maybe he's just a weird guy. Let's ask someone else." Charlie dragged Gabe outside to the man who greeted people as they got on the train.

They ran up to him and Charlie asked, "Excuse me, sir. I was wondering if you knew where Farmers Fresh Meadows was?"

The man tilted his head to the side, just as the ticket man had, and said, "Why would you wanna go there? That's private property. No one is allowed to go around there." The boys took a few steps back.

"Okay, so not just one strange guy," Gabe said while staring off to the distance, thinking. He hit Charlie's chest then asked, "You don't think they're enchanted, do you?"

Charlie rubbed his chest. "First of all, ow, and second, if they are that means we're close to the witches. At least this means Charlie gave us a real address."

"Yeah, but it also means the entire town might be enchanted and we'll never find where Farmer's Fresh Meadows is."

The man who was greeting passengers waved them back over. "Oh, you two are looking for Farmer's Fresh Meadows, huh?"

The boys turned to each other, then back to the man, and nodded. He put one hand in his pocket and used the other to point down the road. "Well, that's not too far from here. You go down that way a bit then take the first right when you reach a fork in the road, and you keep walking till you see the sign."

"Uh, thank you, sir," Gabe said.

They walked away and got a little down the road before Charlie said, "That was weird. That was weird, right?"

"Definitely weird."

They glanced down the road and noticed there were no forks in sight.

"Well, I guess we got a long way to go," Charlie said. "At least we're almost done, then we can relax for eternity."

Gabe wished his transition meant relaxation, but he knew things would probably get worse before they got better.

The boys walked for a mile in the scalding September heat. The kind you get right before it cools down. If they were home, they'd be at the neighborhood pool, sliding down the slide, relaxing on floats. Charlie would try to convince Gabe to play

Marco Polo, and Gabe would say no because the first time they played Charlie almost accidentally drowned Gabe. Normal kid stuff.

Instead, they were here, walking down a dirt road with no end in sight, about to ask a witch to turn them into something Gabe didn't even know existed twenty-four hours before. He rubbed the back of his neck and glanced at the sun. It was already mid-morning, meaning his father had probably gone to check on him, meaning he knew he was missing. He felt like the world's worst child, leaving his papa. Especially after a night like they had. Maybe he should've left a note. He knew it didn't matter. His father would be worried about him no matter what the note said.

Charlie placed his hand over his eyes and grinned, pointing down the road. "I think I see the fork." He grabbed Gabe's arm, and they ran to where the road diverged three ways, straight, left, and right. Charlie made two Ls with his hands before pointing to the left. "That's right."

Gabe shook his head. He didn't want to destroy Charlie's confidence, but he also couldn't spend a few hours walking down a road, only for Charlie to realize they went the wrong way. He grabbed Charlie's arm and pointed to the right.

"Actually, that is."

Charlie dropped his arm. "Whatever, dude, let's just go."

They went down the road, Charlie keeping his eyes peeled for the sign while Gabe distracted himself by kicking every big rock he came across. They walked and walked until they reached the end of the road.

"Huh?" Charlie asked as he looked around. "I never saw a sign." He hit Gabe's shoulder. "Are you sure we went the right way?"

"Uh…" Gabe said. He was never completely confident in his decisions even though he'd known the difference between right and left since he was three years old. "I'm pretty sure."

"Well, I guess I must've missed it. Maybe it was smaller than I imagined."

They headed back down the street. Gabe kept his head up this time, looking everywhere for the sign. When they got halfway back, Gabe's eyes widened as he pointed to the side of the road. "Look."

Charlie looked at the sign and squinted. "What?"

Gabe couldn't believe his friend had missed the sign on their first way down. It was at least ten feet tall and twenty feet wide. They wanted to make sure people knew it was there.

"I don't get what you wanted me to look at. A bird? I don't see any," Charlie said, looking above and below the sign.

Gabe didn't have time for his friend's antics. Charlie had either lost his vision or was playing a cruel joke on him, which Gabe was not happy about. His stomach had been growling for hours. He hoped these witch farm people had some sort of fruit stand.

Gabe held two fingers in front of his friend's eyes. "How many fingers am I holding up?"

Charlie placed his hands on his hips. "Two, like the number of brain cells you have."

Okay, Gabe was starting to grow concerned for his friend. Somehow, he was missing the extremely obvious, large enough to be seen by planes flying by, sign. He did the only thing he could think of. He ran under the sign and pointed above his head.

"This, look."

Charlie glanced above Gabe's head and stared right at the sign.

"What?" he asked, annoyed.

Gabe rubbed his forehead. After this, he was going to need a long nap and a cold soda. He wrapped his legs around the post that held up the sign and said, "Okay, look at me."

"Why are you standing like that?"

"Like what?"

Charlie pretended to wrap his arms around an invisible pole.

"He can't see any of this," a high-pitched voice behind Gabe said, making him scream and fall to the ground.

"Gabe!" Charlie shouted as he ran over to help him, but Gabe was too distracted by the girl standing next to him.

She was about their age, wearing a white, flowy dress, and a floral crown. She had long, white hair, but not in an old lady way, more like Jack Frost style. Some was braided while the rest flowed free. Gabe was completely focused on her.

Charlie, on the other hand, didn't seem to notice she was there. He knelt beside Gabe and held his hand out to help him stand.

"What happened?" He chuckled. "Did you get scared by a squirrel?"

Gabe ignored Charlie and stared at the girl. "Who are you and what do you mean he can't see this?"

Charlie frowned and looked at the girl, but it was more like he was looking through her.

She smiled. "We enchanted this property to keep our coven safe from other witches." She held her hand out. Once he grabbed it, she helped him stand, which only confused Charlie more. He stood and stared at his hand Gabe hadn't grabbed.

"Okay, what's going on?" Charlie asked, making the girl giggle.

Gabe looked between them. "Can you explain what is happening right now?" he asked the girl.

"This is my home. We are a coven of witches who use our powers to grow herbs and cast spells on the locals who may come to us injured. I've even healed a cracked skull." She smiled like it was the coolest thing she'd ever done. Gabe agreed. That was pretty cool.

"While that's awesome, why can't my friend see anything?"

The girl frowned. "A long time ago, many years before I was born, an evil coven of witches came to my family's home and poisoned all the crops. We didn't know until it was too late. Many people died, including my great-grandmother. It made the town want to hunt and kill the witches they'd previously called their friends, so my family ran here and cast a spell on the land so that only humans would be able to see the property."

Gabe nodded as though any of that sounded normal. Apparently, witches, good and evil, have been around as long as humans and they even had their own little witch wars.

"Okay, I guess that makes sense, but what does that have to do with my friend?" Gabe asked as Charlie waved a hand in front of his face.

"Hello, what are you doing?" Charlie asked.

The girl looked at Charlie as though he were a dog chasing his tail "Look, I'm sure your friend is a good person, but we don't allow witches—"

"Woah, woah, woah!" Gabe said, holding his hands out. "My friend isn't a witch." He glanced over at Charlie as he threw himself across Gabe's eyeline, through the pole Gabe had just held onto. "How did you do that?" Gabe asked the girl.

She shrugged. "The magical barrier around the village noticed your friend was supernatural and makes anything he comes into contact with temporarily disappear. All he sees is an empty field with a few trees, nothing more."

Charlie stood, dusted a few leaves off his shirt, then stared at Gabe concerned. "Gabe," he said, "I think we need to go home and talk to your dad."

Gabe inhaled a sharp breath. He gently grabbed the girl's arm and said, "Please, you have to let my friend see you."

The girl shook her head. "I'm sorry, I cannot. My coven would hate me. No other witch had seen us here since we moved."

Charlie grabbed Gabe's arm and tried to pull him back to the road. "Come on, buddy. I see it, I do, but right now I think we should go home."

Gabe could tell Charlie was lying and still didn't see what was right in front of him.

"Please," he said, deciding to beg the girl one last time. "You don't understand. My mom is sick. She sees things that aren't there sometimes, and now my friend's gonna think I'm sick and make us go home and make my dad worried. Please let him see. Then if you tell us to leave, we'll leave."

Charlie's eyes were starting to water. "Come on, please, Gabe. We can do this another time."

The girl stared at Charlie. She placed her hand on his chest, and her eyes started to glow. She checked behind her then snapped her fingers in front of Charlie's face.

Charlie's jaw dropped as his arms fell by his side. "Uh," he said as he stared at the girl. He wiped away the tears on his sleeve and said, "Uh, hello."

The girl continued to check behind her, making sure they were alone, before pushing the boys to the road. "See, you both have seen me, now leave."

Charlie, who'd only just joined the conversation, dug his heels into the ground, preventing her from pushing them away. "What do you mean? Who are you? What's going on?"

"We do not allow witches from other covens to come here. I'm sorry, but you'll have to leave," she said.

"But we're not witches," Charlie said, making the girl freeze.

"You mean you don't know?" she asked.

Charlie and Gabe turned to the girl.

"Know what?" Gabe asked.

"Oh, I've never met a witch who didn't know they were a witch," she said, staring in amazement at Charlie.

He pointed to himself. "You mean, me? I'm a witch?" He shook his head. "I'm not a witch." He placed his hand over his mouth. "Am I?"

The girl tilted her head to the side and smiled. "Were you adopted?"

Charlie shook his head. "I wish."

"Hmm, and you've never done anything strange? Out of the ordinary?"

Charlie thought it over. "No, I mean, besides being the best swimmer on my swim team."

Gabe hit his arm. "And the twirly leaf thing you do."

Charlie shrugged. "Yeah, but that was just a spell my great-grandpa had taught me." He picked a leaf off his shirt and placed it in his palm, making it twirl and explode.

The girl stared at them as though they were the dumbest people she'd ever met. Like they'd gone on a lengthy discussion about how two plus two is twenty-seven.

"You're saying you can do a spell, but you still didn't know you were a witch?"

Well, when she put it like that, it did make them seem rather dumb, Gabe thought.

"But I thought everyone could do simple spells. Like witches were people who had like, big powers and stuff, or could control different elements like avatar," Charlie explained.

The girl picked up a leaf and placed it in Gabe's hand. "Make it float," she said.

Gabe pointed to the leaf, but it didn't move. "I can't."

"Exactly, because you're not a witch." She brushed her palms together. "My work here is done." She turned the boys around and continued to push them to the street. "Now leave."

"Hold on," Charlie said. "I just found out some life-changing news, and I need a minute."

"Take all the time you need." Charlie smiled until she continued. "I'm sure you have a long walk home. You can process it on your way."

She turned around and headed back to the field, but Charlie wasn't finished speaking with her. "I found out that not only have I been practicing magic for years—"

"Performing one spell is not practicing magic. You wouldn't say you were practicing piano if you played the same key every day," she said.

Charlie waved his hands in the air as Gabe reluctantly followed. "Fine, I find out I've been robbed of the opportunity to practice magic for years, and now you expect me to what? Leave?"

"Yes!" the girl shouted then turned to make sure no one heard her. "That is exactly what I expect you to do because that is what your friend said you would do, and I don't take kindly to people breaking promises."

"Charlie, I did say we would leave," said Gabe.

Charlie crossed his arms. "Well, just because my friend was easy to give up doesn't mean I am. I deserve to know more about this witch stuff."

"Ask your parents," she spat.

"Oh, yeah, let me go up to them, after returning from running away from home, and say, hey, Mom and Dad, you know how you hate magic and have been lying to me for thirteen years? Well, now that I know one of you is a witch, you probably will sit me down and have a nice chat, where we hug at the end, right?"

The girl turned and shrugged. "That's how my family solves problems."

He leaned in close, so his face was mere inches from hers and said, "Well, sorry, not everyone can be perfect."

Gabe wasn't sure stepping between two witches when they were angry was a good idea, but he also didn't want them making each other so mad they got into a fight. Charlie would do his one-leaf trick, and she would use her powers to blast him into another town.

He slipped between his best friend and the girl and said, "Okay, let's calm down. Why don't we take a breath and talk?"

"Yes, let's," an older voice from behind them said. They all turned to stare at the woman with wide eyes, but the girl looked the most nervous.

"Mother, what are you doing here? I thought you'd gone to town."

The woman, who was wearing normal street clothing, a pair of jeans and a white, loose button-up top with a tank top underneath, crossed her arms. "Maria, do you want to tell me why there is a witch in our yard?"

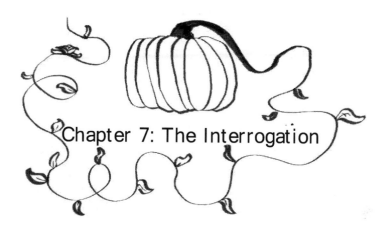

Chapter 7: The Interrogation

Maria tried to explain what had happened, but her mother held up her index finger to stop her.

"Hush." She turned to Gabe and Charlie. "Follow me."

The three kids followed her through the long fields of luscious, green grass until they got to the edge of a cliff. The boys looked down and gulped before taking a step back.

"Uh, ma'am, please, don't throw us over," Gabe pleaded. "This is all my fault."

"No, it's not," Charlie said. Gabe sighed, happy his friend was defending him, until Charlie pointed to Maria and said, "It's her fault." She glared at him with crossed arms.

Gabe sighed; he was too young to die.

The older woman shook her head and waved her hand. Everyone floated into the air. They went up and over the edge before slowly gliding to the ground.

"This is a shortcut," she said.

The boys had never felt so weightless. It was as though their feet were touching a floor of some sort, but there was nothing but air under them. Gabe always thought flying would make him want to throw up since he got motion sick in cars and on boats. Instead, he felt free, as if he were swimming but without the water pushing him around. Charlie grinned as their feet gently landed on the grass below.

"Awesome," he said.

Now that they were on the ground, they could clearly see their surroundings. There were miles of fruits, vegetables, and herbs growing tall and beautifully throughout the garden. Dozens of women of all ages were scattered among the plants. The young girls were running their hands inches above the weeds till they disappeared, and the older women were twirling their fingers and singing, making the plants double in size.

The oldest woman was reading a book to a pumpkin about the size of Cinderella's cart. The vines curled around her but not in a threatening way more like a young child hanging off their grandmother's shoulders.

"Whoa," Gabe said when he noticed who, or more like what, was watering the garden. Three scarecrows were going around every plant sprinkling water from watering cans.

They took a step forward, and every witch, besides Maria and her mom, turned to look at the two boys. The oldest woman dropped her book and made her way over with a scowl on her face.

"What is he doing here?" the old woman asked, hobbling over to Charlie. Before she could touch him, Maria's mom held out her hand and stopped her.

"Mom, please. I've got this." The older woman stared at them for a moment before shaking her head and going back to her pumpkin. Maria's mother turned to Gabe and waved for him to keep following her. They walk through the garden paths, trying not to stare when a scarecrow walked by and spilled a little water on Charlie's foot.

At the end of the garden was a circle of houses. They must've been built by hand. They had mud walls and no doors. Gabe guessed they had nothing to keep out. Maria's mother stopped at the second house on the left.

"Right this way, boys," she said.

Gabe and Charlie stood close as they made their way through the doorway. Maria tried to follow, but her mother stopped her.

"No. This is a discussion I must have alone." She narrowed her eyes. "I will be having a discussion with you later. Go help your sisters with the weeding."

Maria slumped her shoulders. "But Mom—-" She stopped when her mother gave her the look. You know, the "I'm really disappointed in you and I don't think you want to push me right now look". "Okay," she said before waving to Gabe and heading away from the house.

The inside was beautiful. The walls were painted a light pink, and there was a hand-carved kitchen table with four chairs around it. The legs were covered with carvings of flying fairies and birds. The top of the table shined so much, Gabe and Charlie could see their own reflection.

"Please sit," Maria's mother said, pointing to the table.

They grabbed two of the chairs and sat beside each other. They scooted the chairs closer together as though their closeness could prevent the witch from making them explode or turn into pumpkins or whatever witches did to intruders.

"Ma'am, I would like to say that we do not know anything about this witch stuff," said Gabe. Charlie opened his mouth to add, but Gabe figured it was better to stop his friend before he could say something to get them in worse trouble. "You see, my friend didn't even know he was a witch until we came here. His family is very secretive and never told him, so please, don't be mad at us."

The woman stood tall. She sighed at the boys. "Very well, but if you two know nothing of magic, then why did you come here?"

Gabe squirmed in his seat, so Charlie took the opportunity to say, "We want to be turned into vampires."

The blinds over the large windows closed magically, the tea kettle started blaring, and the birds that had just landed by the door flew away. The witch placed her hands on the table and said, "I don't know how you boys learned about vampires or who told you how they transformed, but I need you to leave my property and never speak of those horrible creatures again, understand?"

Gabe stood. "Yes, ma'am. Good day." He waved for Charlie, but he stayed seated. "Come on. You promised that if she said no, we'd go home." Gabe didn't know why he wanted to give up so easily. By the time they'd arrived at the farm, he felt in too deep to turn back. He had to transform, had to save his mom, but now that the woman said no, he felt confident in her words, like he could trust her to tell him anything and he'd do it. Wait a minute...

"Hey," Gabe said, "you're enchanting me. That's not very nice." The woman stepped toward him, and all Gabe's newfound confidence diminished. "I mean, I'm sure you're a nice lady. I just—"

She got so close he had to sit back in his seat to move away from her. "Listen here, boys. Becoming a vampire is not like it is in the movies."

"They're not immortal?" Charlie asked.

The witch looked to the side. "Yes, but—"

"They don't drink blood?" Gabe asked.

"Well, they do but—"

"They don't have super speed and super strength?" Charlie asked.

The woman was so upset she was almost foaming at the mouth. "Okay, it's exactly like in the movies!" the woman shouted. "But and it's a very big but—" Both boys started chuckling. "What?" the witch asked.

"You said big butt," Charlie said in the middle of his laughs.

The boys could tell the woman wanted to rip them in half and throw them off over a cliff, but they were suddenly calm. They weren't afraid anymore. Gabe noticed something move out of the corner of his eye, so he turned to the window. That's when he saw Maria waving her hands around as though performing a spell. She must be enchanting them, Gabe thought, but he didn't care.

The witch slammed her fist on the table. "Listen to me. Becoming a vampire is not something you want to do. It's dangerous, and you might not survive."

They stopped laughing.

"What?" Charlie asked.

The witch cleared her throat and then said, "The spell is very dangerous. It takes almost everything a witch has to perform it on one person, let alone two. Besides, I've never met a witch who has performed the spell, and it involves you drinking a special concoction of herbs. You would be given to the earth in a burial, then if, and only if, the ground determines you're worthy, you will come back, but if you don't, you stay dead."

Gabe wasn't so sure of this idea anymore, and he knew it wasn't because of Maria's mother's enchantment. He couldn't do that to his family. He couldn't risk not coming home.

"How likely is that we wouldn't be 'returned to the earth'?" Charlie asked while making air quotations with his fingers.

The witch took a step back and thought it over. "Not likely."

Gabe was ready to go home and find another way to help his mother, but then Charlie said, "Well, that sounds weird because you said you've never known a witch who has performed the spell before, so how would you know how dangerous it was?" He stood and took a step towards the witch, his hands behind his back. "I think you're lying to scare us. I don't think you know how dangerous it is." He took another step closer. "I think you just want us to leave."

Maria's mother's mouth stayed open as though she'd been petrified. She must not have expected some child to outthink her.

Gabe sat back and stared at his friend, again surprised he would talk like that to a powerful supernatural creature. His friend wasn't very confrontational. Sure, he could take on another thirteen-year-old in a fist fight, but he would usually stutter and sweat when trying to lie to adults. Somehow, in the last twenty-four hours, he developed a newfound confidence in talking to people who could do much worse than give him detention.

The witch was only caught off guard for a moment before she stood, wiped off her dress, and pointed to the door. "I want you both to leave now."

Gabe grabbed Charlie's arm and dragged him out of the woman's house. "So sorry," he said as he pushed Charlie out the door. "My friend isn't usually like this. He's tired and hungry. So... okay bye." He shoved Charlie to the path.

Charlie fought against Gabe, but in the end, Gabe won.

"Come on, man. Why can't we leave? It was a dumb idea, and I wanna go home and eat," Gabe begged.

"I've got something you can eat if you want to follow me."

They turned to see Maria standing on the path behind them, fingers intertwined as she swung back and forth.

Gabe raised his brow as Charlie asked, "Is this a trick? You take us in for food, and it's actually poisoned?"

She giggled and waved her hand. The boys followed her down the path, crouching down as they passed Maria's mother's house. At the end of the path was a tiny hut, like a playhouse version of the others. She pushed aside the curtain that guarded the door and waited for them to go in before closing the curtain behind them. In the tiny hut was a small wooden table with only one chair, bags of herbs tied to hooks on the wall, and a rolled-up mat with blankets folded over it lying on the floor.

"This is my hut. Every witch in our coven gets one when they come of age," she explained as the boys looked around.

"Wait, how old are you?" Charlie asked.

"Thirteen," she said as she crossed her legs on the ground. "That's when you start learning more dangerous magic. My aunts have taught me many things in the past month."

She moved the blankets aside to reveal a hand stitch book. "But nothing has taught me as much as this." She ran her fingers over the leather cover and

stared as though enchanted with the Latin letters
carved in the front. She placed the book in the middle
of the room and waited until Gabe and Charlie sat
around it to open it. She flipped through the pages
until she revealed one that read, 'Lamia Transmutatio
Carmine'.

"Here," she said, pointing to the page.

Charlie raised his hand as though he were in class
before asking, "What does that mean? We can't read
gibberish."

She sent him a cold glare. "It's Latin, and it reads
vampire transformation spell. I believe this is what you
came for."

Both boys nodded. Gabe grabbed his shoe-covered
toes and leaned forward, as though the closer he got to
the book, the easier it'd be to read. He ran his fingers
down the page. Under the multiple instructions were at
least 12 different items. He recognized a few of them
as scientific names for herbs.

"Are these the ingredients?" he asked.

She nodded. "I do not have all of them. I don't
think anyone in the village carries these two," she said
while pointing to the bottom ones on the list. "Which
doesn't matter because they would know if I took
something from them, and they cannot know about
this." She stared at Charlie then Gabe "Promise?"

Gabe still didn't like the idea. Maybe Maria's
mother was lying, and she didn't know how dangerous
the spell might be, but she could still be right. It could
still be dangerous. Maybe it would be better to leave
before things got too dangerous to turn back.

Charlie must've noticed his anxiety because he bumped Gabe's shoulder and said, "Hey, it's gonna be okay. I'll make sure we return home in one piece, I promise. Do you trust me?"

That question pulled Gabe into a memory of the first time they met, which was also the first time Charlie had asked him that very same question.

Charlie had told him that keeping his training wheels on his bike was keeping him from having fun. Gabe told him they were keeping him safe, but Charlie said they weren't and that he was depending on the wheels, not himself, and that was more dangerous.

Gabe didn't believe him and took off down the hill on their street. Halfway down, he had grown nervous and stumbled. When he got to the end, his heart jolted and he tried to break, but his front tire caught the sidewalk, and he was thrown over the bike.

After Charlie had made sure he was okay, he asked if he could take the training wheels off Gabe's bike. Gabe was hesitant, but Charlie had told him to trust him. Gabe told him to remove the wheels, thinking he would grab a screwdriver to take them off. Instead, Charlie held the bike high and hit the training wheel against the sidewalk, making it break off. He did it again on the other side then pushed the bike to Gabe.

They walked back up the hill and stared at the bottom. Gabe's nerves were worse than before, and he didn't know if he'd be okay falling again. Charlie had told him to believe in himself, and he would be okay. He tried, and even when he got scared, he believed things would be okay. When they skidded to the end safely, they hopped off their bikes and shouted with joy.

His trusting Charlie made it so he didn't have to use training wheels anymore. Though sometimes his trust had landed them in bad places, even in-school suspension, Charlie always had his back. Together they could get turned and get home in one piece. They would make it through, especially now that they had a witch on their side—which made him think...

"Why are you helping us? Your mom said this was a bad idea and dangerous for you."

Maria bit her lip and looked away. "Well, I knew if we let you leave, you would do something stupid like trying to perform the spell on yourself. The book says that would lead to your death and possibly an explosion from an untrained witch, and you," she said while looking at Charlie, "are very untrained."

Charlie slumped his shoulders. He did not like being reminded of how he was never given training for something no one ever told him he was. "Also, I read through the spell multiple times. There have only been three cases of people not being returned from the earth. And it was two old guys and some girl who was a werewolf, but neither of you are werewolves, are you?"

They shook their heads, but from all Gabe's learned in the past 24 hours, he might just be waiting for the day he transforms into a four-legged beast under the light of the full moon.

"Good. The only issue we have is getting these last few ingredients," she said, pointing to the bottom of the list.

Charlie stood and gave her a thumbs up. "Great. We can order them and have them delivered in like two days max."

Maria placed her hand on his shoulder and lowered him back to the floor. "No, you have to collect them from where they naturally grow. Luckily, there is one place they all grow and are currently in blooming season."

That was lucky, Gabe thought.

"Where?" he asked.

Maria shifted onto her knees and said, "Hokkaido, Japan."

Chapter 8: The Lesson

Both boys groaned.

"How are we supposed to get to Japan? We don't even have passports, and even if we did, we couldn't afford plane tickets," Charlie complained.

"Yes, and that would be a problem," she said, flipping through the book until she found the page she was looking for, "if there wasn't a portal spell." On the page were three instructions, and next to them was a picture of a black circle with glowing lights around it. "If I cast a spell, I can portal you anywhere in the world, but once you get there, I don't know if I'll have enough power to move you around or get you back."

Gabe did not like how many obstacles they had come across on their quest. It's as if the universe was telling them to turn back, but they'd found a solution to every problem so far. They had to have one for this.

Gabe snapped his fingers. "Got it. Teach the spell to Charlie, and he can portal us home."

Maria bit her lip. She did not seem to have a lot of competence in Charlie's abilities, but there was no other way, so she nodded. "Okay, this is pretty basic stuff once you get the hang of it." She stood and held her hand out. "Now, come on. We must hurry. If I'm not out in the fields by dinner, they'll come looking for me, and things will not be good for any of us, but especially you."

Gabe grabbed her hand, and they followed her out of the hut, checking both ways before running away from the cabin and into the dark woods. He did not like being in the woods. He wished they could have stayed back in the bright cabin, but no, they had to train in a place he was sure was swarming with dangerous animals. He crossed his fingers behind his back and whispered, "Please no mountain lions. Please no mountain lions."

They got to a clearing in the trees where there was thankfully a slight ray of sunshine to lighten up the area. Maria held her hands palms out and facing up. Charlie placed his over top of hers. She closed her eyes and took a deep breath. The trees around them flooded with birds, some beautiful colors of orange, red, and green. Others were majestic blackbirds that swept under the branches and surrounded their heads.

Maria's eyes opened wide, and she pulled back so fast she fell.

"What? What's wrong?" Charlie asked as he held out his hand to help her. She took it and shook her head. Her eyes filled with wonder and curiosity.

"Usually, un-trained witches have a small amount of untapped power that will grow with training, but you are already filled to the brim with energy. You have magic coursing through your every vein as though you've been training since birth."

Charlie gulped. He knew that was not the case. The only spell he'd ever been taught was the one with the leaf by his great-grandfather on one of their very few trips to visit him.

He'd been only four years old. His parents wanted to visit his great-grandfather, but Charlie had wanted to do anything else. His great-grandfather had been stuck in a bed Charlie's entire life. They only visited him a few times a year, and he couldn't play or even stay awake long enough to have fun conversations. Plus, the old man was always sad.

Charlie sat in the hard, plastic hospital chair and listened to his mother and father shout with his great-grandfather. Charlie assumed his great-grandfather must've done something really bad to always get yelled at. When the shouting got louder, Charlie turned to stare at the floor. He knew if his father saw him crying, he would tell him not to be a baby.

A woman wearing a light green pair of scrubs walked in and waved his parents outside. Charlie got up to follow them, but his father held out his palm and said, "Wait here. We'll be right back." Charlie frowned. He didn't want to be alone with the old man he barely knew.

"Charlie?" his great-grandfather asked. Charlie slowly turned around, surprised to see the old man smiling. "Come sit by me."

Charlie felt a little less scared now that his great-grandfather seemed to be happier. Charlie understood. He was always happier when his parents stopped yelling at him too. He sat back in his chair and crossed his legs. That's when he noticed the leaf stuck to the bottom of the shoe. He pulled it off and was going to drop it to the floor when his great-grandfather held his hand out.

"Give it here. I want to show you something."

Charlie had no idea what he could possibly show him about the leaf that was cool, but old people were weird. They would forget your name or tell you the same story over and over again.

Charlie gave him the leaf. His great-grandfather placed the leaf on his palm and then checked behind them to make sure no one was going to reenter the room before twirling his fingers over the leaf. Charlie couldn't believe his eyes as the leaf lifted off his grandfather's hand and flew in the air.

"Whoa, how did you do that?" Charlie asked.

His grandfather smiled so wide his eyes crinkled. "Magic and you can do it too."

Charlie pointed to himself. "Me?"

His great grandfather chuckled as he nodded. "Yes, let me show you." He gently took Charlie's hand and held his palm up then placed the leaf on it. He took Charlie's other hand and said, "Now the motion is to swirl your finger like this," he said as he moved his finger in a clockwise rotation, "and then pick it up. You have to see yourself doing it in your mind, first. You must know how to do it before you can do it, understand?"

Charlie was four, so no, he didn't understand. But he'd watched his great-grandfather do it, and he figured he'd give it a go.

"Now don't be sad when you don't get it on your first try. It took me seventeen tr—" His great-grandfather was silenced as he watched the leaf fly into the air. "My goodness," he whispered.

Charlie had no trouble keeping the leaf high in the air. He turned to his great-grandfather and giggled as the leaf landed on his bald head. His great-grandfather took the leaf and gave it back to Charlie then said, "You are a very special boy, Charlie, but let's make sure we keep this to ourselves for now. When you get older..." He looked at the necklace that laid under his hospital gown. "Well, when you get older, I probably won't be here."

"Where will you be?" Charlie asked as he placed a leaf on his forehead.

The old man gave him a warm smile. "It doesn't matter, but when you get older, I want you to track down your Nanny Jo. Do you remember her from my birthday party?" He did. She was cool and always brought candy and funny stories. Charlie liked her. "Okay. When you get older, I want you to go to her and show her your cool trick. Tell her I told you that you were really special. Okay?"

Charlie nodded with a proud smile. No one had ever called him special before. It felt nice, like his great grandfather meant it.

He never got to contact Jo since she passed away around the same time as his great-grandfather, but he never forgot that day. The day he learned he was special. He'd always thought his great-grandfather meant it in a: you're my great-grandkid, so I think you're special because we're related kind of way, but he was starting to think the old man had meant in a magical way.

"Well, this should be easier than I hoped," Maria said as she held her hands out again, this time towards the space between the trees, and made a circular motion. "Do this and say the word, saperta porta, ut locum puto."

The leaves on the ground started flying into the air as a black portal opened then, in the circle, a Dippin' Dots appeared.

"Whoa, I love Dippin' Dots. You can go there whenever you want?" Gabe asked.

She shrugged. "Not if my mother catches me, so hurry. Try to think of someplace and make it appear."

Charlie held his hands up and swirled them in a circular motion. He said the words, and a portal appeared.

"Wow, impressive!" Maria said as she waited for the place to appear. The black portal contorted into a tall bookstore with a blue panel roof and a paint splatter door.

"What is that?" Gabe asked.

Charlie shrugged. "I don't know. I've always dreamed about this place. I wanted to see if it was real."

"Makes sense that it is. Your mind takes the places you've seen before and smashes them together when it makes dreams," Gabe explained.

"Yeah, but I've never been to a house like this. At least I don't remember," said Charlie as he stared at the portal.

"Sometimes our subconscious remembers things that our conscious mind doesn't," said Maria "When you return, we can meditate on this, but now you have to go." She handed them a small light brown leather bag. "This has many herbs that will help you on your journey. I labeled them because I didn't think you'd be able to remember them all. Some of them are to calm you down in times of fear. Others are for healing. You only need a small amount to do either, so don't waste them on a paper cut or bee sting, okay?" They nodded, deciding to let her teasing go since she was risking so much to help them.

She opened another glowing portal. "You will find your first ingredient here. This will help you know what to look for and where to go next." She handed them a rolled-up scroll.

Gabe unrolled it, and a map appeared with a picture of a plant sketched on the corner. The sketched plant flew back and forth as though it were flowing in the wind. "I'll be controlling the map from here. Create a portal to contact me when you're done, and I'll change it for the next ingredient."

She stepped back so the boys would have enough room to get through.

Charlie stopped before taking a step towards the portal. He grabbed Gabe's arm and asked, "Are you sure about this?"

Gabe nodded. He was nervous, but he needed to try for his mom. Charlie threw the bag over his shoulder, and Gabe clenched the scroll. They turned to each other, then to the portal, and took a step inside.

Chapter 9: The Light Becomes Night

It felt like someone grabbed their ankles and pulled them through the rest of the portal before throwing them to the other side.

"Ow," Charlie said as he rubbed his head and sat up.

"Uh, Charlie," Gabe said, looking around. "We have a problem."

Charlie, whose eyes had been closed due to the pounding pain in his forehead, opened his eyes. He was surprised to see it was as dark as when they were closed.

"Japan is never this dark in anime," Charlie said as he looked around at the pitch-black scenery.

Gabe slapped his forehead. "I completely forgot about the time difference. Japan is thirteen hours ahead of where we came from. It's the middle of the night. Crap."

Charlie placed the bag beside him and felt around until he found a long, metal stick. He pressed the button on the stick's side and a light appeared.

"At least we have these," he said as he held up his flashlight. "Now, let's go find some ingredients."

They jumped to their feet and followed the map. It glowed, so they didn't need to shine the flashlight to see it. On the map was a tiny dot that moved whenever they moved. Attached to the dot was a line, and at the other end of the line was an X. It was as if they were pirates looking for buried treasure.

They realized they were in the middle of a wide forest on the side of a mountain. They had to go slow to keep themselves from falling forward and tumbling down the hill. Under their feet leaves crunched and sticks snapped. Gabe tensed whenever they made a sound because it signaled to the creatures in the woods that they were there.

The temperature had dropped since they went from a warm-weather state in mid-morning to a night in another country. The gentle breeze wiped away the sweat from Gabe's forehead and helped him feel less lightheaded. He still needed food, but he figured he could make it a few more hours before the hunger started to take over and make him feel bad.

"Hey, look, I think I found it!" Charlie shouted as he pointed his flashlight at a plant.

The plant was spread out along the side of the hill, near a trail. There were multiple flowers that looked like dandelions when they turned white, but these were purple. They grew in bunches, off tiny twigs that had three-point, green leaves along their sides.

"Alright, I'm gonna grab some," Charlie said as he reached for the plant.

Before he could touch the flower, Gabe shouted, "Stop!"

Charlie froze. "What?"

"It could be poisonous," said Gabe.

Charlie placed his hands on his hips. "Why would Maria send us to collect poisonous plants?"

"I don't know. She's a witch. They probably use some dangerous ingredients. Neither of us are good enough at herbology to know. It's better to be safe than sorry," Gabe said as he handed Charlie a small, plastic bag from their sack.

Charlie turned the bag inside out, so it wrapped around his hand. He reached for the plant, keeping the rest of his body as far away as possible and, as though he were picking up a piece of dog poop off the ground, grabbed for the flower.

He zipped it up, making sure his fingers stayed away from any place the plant touched then threw the bag into their sack.

Charlie sighed and wiped his hands. "There, done. Onto the next one."

Right after he said that, the world became dark. Charlie hit his flashlight a few times, but it stayed off.

"The batteries must've died," he said as he placed it back into their sack. "Maybe the map can light our way?"

Gabe turned the map around, but the light emitting from it only shined a few inches in front of them.

"Well, that's not good," Charlie said with a shrug of the shoulders as though it weren't a big deal. As though they weren't stranded in the middle of the mountain woods in a country they didn't know much about. As though it wasn't midnight.

Gabe did not like this one bit. He kept the map close to his chest, so he could at least have a small amount of light, but it wasn't enough. He had no idea what was lurking in these woods, and now a creature could come and attack him before he even realized something was behind him.

"Well, I think we should sleep. Looks like we have a long walk ahead of us," Charlie said, pointing to the map.

He was right. The line between the dot and the new X was much longer than the first one had been. It looked like they were going to have to walk halfway across the island. Gabe's legs grew weak at the thought of all that walking. Sleeping for a bit, at least until the sun came up, sounded like a great idea.

Except the sleeping in the scary woods part. How would they protect themselves if they were asleep? Then again, how would they protect themselves if they were awake? They couldn't fight off a bear or a mountain lion. They probably couldn't even fight off a squirrel though Gabe would never admit it out loud.

"Okay, let's sleep by a tree though, so at least one part of us can be protected," Gabe suggested. They had a long day ahead of them, and they would need at least another few hours of rest since the train bathroom had been less than peaceful.

They got to a tall, thick tree and laid their sack beside it. It was a long bag, so they placed their heads on either side and closed their eyes.

Charlie was able to fall asleep in minutes. Gabe had a much harder time. Every time he'd hear a sound his eyes would shoot open and glance around as though he'd suddenly develop night vision.

He wrapped his arms around his chest, giving himself a hug, hoping the pressure would calm him down. It didn't. He laid the map in his chest like it were a blanket and stared at the stars dancing in the sky.

That's when he remembered the phone in his pocket.

He slipped it out and sighed when the screen lit up. He frowned when he noticed he only had two percent battery. He hoped it would give him enough light to lull him to sleep, but then he had a better idea.

He sat up and placed his back against the tree, dialing a few numbers into the phone. It rang a few times before his father answered.

"Hello?" he said with a voice more tired than Gabe had ever heard.

"Papa?" Gabe whispered, to not wake Charlie.

"Mi Hijo, where are you? What happened? Are you okay?" His father asked so fast, Gabe could barely understand what he said.

"I'm okay, Papa. I promise," Gabe said.

"Where are you? Come home right now. No, stay there, and I'll come pick you up." His father sounded like he had tears in his eyes, which made Gabe's stomach ache. He'd never made his father cry before.

"I'll be home soon, I promise. I'm doing something that will help Mom. I can't tell you where I am, but I will be safe," Gabe said.

"That doesn't make any sense, Gabe. You tell me where you are right now," his father demanded. "I will come get you, and I can help you with whatever it is you are doing."

"I love you, Papa," Gabe said before hanging up the phone.

He placed the phone beside his head and stared at the now lit-up tree limbs above him. A tear rolled from his eye to his hair. He felt horrible for making his father so worried, but it would be worth it in the end. He could help his family, and everything would be okay.

He closed his eyes and drifted to sleep as the phone buzzed and turned off, leaving them alone in the dark woods.

Chapter 10: The Beary Serious Situation

Gabe was awoken to the sound of his stomach growling so loud, he could barely hear Charlie giggling beside him. Man, he wished he'd remembered to ask Maria for the food she'd told them she had.

"Stop licking me, Sprinkles," Charlie said through his laughter.

Sprinkles? That was the name of Gabe's Nana's cat. Charlie loved to play with her when she visited, but there was no way Sprinkles had gotten to Japan. Gabe turned over and saw what his dreaming friend was mistaking for a sweet cat. He screamed.

Standing next to Charlie, not much bigger than a dog, was a fluffy, brown, baby bear.

The bear looked up at him, his tongue still sticking out, slobbering all over Charlie's hair. Gabe kicked Charlie's side.

"Dude, wake up."

Charlie groaned but opened his eyes. "Ew," he said as he placed his fingers into his wet hair. "What's this?"

Gabe shook Charlie's shoulder then pointed to the baby bear, who was sitting beside Charlie, smiling. Charlie looked at where Gabe was pointing and screamed, backing away and bumping into his friend.

"That's a bear," Charlie said nervously. Then he smiled. "Aww, it's a baby." Charlie reached his hand out to pet the bear when Gabe grabbed his arm.

"Yeah, that's a bad idea." He held Charlie's hands back as he tried to wiggle free.

"Come on, it's a little baby. Look how small his nose is." Charlie got one hand free and reached out to touch the bear's nose. Gabe slapped his hand. "OW!" Charlie screamed.

"I thought you were supposed to be the animal expert. You know that messing with baby bears only leads to mama bear showing up and tearing you up into little pieces," Gabe said. He picked up a leaf and tore it apart as an example.

"But look at the little fella," Charlie said, pushing out his bottom lip to pout. Gabe glanced at the baby bear, but all he saw were its vicious teeth and claws.

"You promised we'd get back in one piece, Charlie." Gabe held up his pointing finger. "One piece."

Charlie sighed. "Okay, fine." He reached for the bag. "It is weird he would come this close to us. Usually, baby bears are taught to fear huma—oh, no!" he said as he looked in the bag.

"What?" Gabe asked as he leaned over, still keeping an eye on the bear.

Charlie lifted a torn-up plastic bag out of the sack. Written on it was, 'Calming Herbs'. The bag was empty.

They turned to the bear, who was still sitting, staring at them without a care in the world. On his chin was a tiny, green stem.

"Oh, that makes more sense," Charlie said as he smiled at the bear. He placed the empty bag back into the sack and looked through it. "Phew, we still have the healing herbs. Those are the most important."

Gabe agreed. He could calm himself down if he needed, but he couldn't heal wounds by deep breathing exercises.

"Okay, we should get going. We don't have any time to waste, and it would be better to leave before his mama shows up," Gabe said. They got to their feet, and Charlie waved to the bear.

"Bye, be safe little guy." They turned and started walking away but only made it a few feet when they noticed the bear was following them.

They stopped and turned around. Charlie kneeled and pointed behind the bear. "You need to stay here. Go find your mama."

Gabe rolled his eyes. It was obvious the bear had no idea what Charlie was saying. It walked up to Charlie's hand and started licking it, making Charlie giggle again.

"No, no, no. We gotta go, bye." Charlie stood, and they started walking again. The bear stayed seated as Gabe focused on the map.

"Okay, so the map says we have to get to a town call—" Gabe stopped when he saw Charlie's cheeks grow red. "He's following us, isn't he?"

"Pfff, no," Charlie lied. Gabe had no idea how Charlie could confront dangerous supernaturals but not say a simple no without smiling when it came to lying to him.

"Uh-huh." Gabe turned around to see the bear right behind them. "No," he said while kneeling beside the bear and pointing at himself. "I go; you stay." The bear nudged his nose against Gabe's knee. "This is pointless." He stood and kept walking. "He can follow us. Hopefully, the calming herbs will wear off soon, and he will get scared and run away."

They continued walking towards the path with the bear bumping into the back of their legs every few seconds. Every time he'd hit Charlie's leg, he'd laugh. When he hit Gabe's leg, he would grip the map a little tighter and frown.

They were five steps away from the trail when Charlie grabbed Gabe's arm to stop him. Gabe looked up from his map and rolled his eyes. "What now?"

Charlie pointed to their right, where the side of the mountain dipped. Laying on its side was a fully-grown, brown bear.

"Do you think that's his mama?" Charlie asked. Before Gabe could answer, the baby bear ran from behind their legs to the big bear. The little one placed his paws on the big one's face, right next to the bear's unusual, upturned snout. When the bigger bear stayed still, the little one nudged it with his nose, as though trying to wake it up.

"Do you think she's okay?" Charlie asked as his lip wobbled.

Oh, no, Gabe thought, this was not good. Charlie always had a soft spot for animals. Once, a puppy was running around Charlie's front yard. He thought it must've been a stray because it had no collar, so he ran out to grab it and take it inside. That's when he found out it was a baby fox, not a dog. That was also the day he received his first series of many rabies shots. He showed off his band-aids to Gabe, but he wasn't upset he was wrong. He didn't mind the scratches that covered his face and arms. He was worried about what they would do to the fox.

"What if they hurt him because he hurt me?" he had asked Gabe that night as they slept in a tent on Gabe's floor. "It wasn't his fault. I shouldn't have tried to play with him."

Maybe his friend felt invincible since he'd recently received another set of rabies shots, but they couldn't protect him from getting torn apart. Charlie started heading towards the bear, but before he could make it a step, Gabe grabbed his arm and pulled him towards the trail.

"Leave the bear. It's the circle of life, Charlie. We've both seen the Lion King," Gabe said. He wasn't heartless. The thought of leaving a baby bear with a dying or possibly deceased mother was heart wrenching, but they couldn't do anything about it.

"We can give it CPR," Charlie suggested as he watched the baby bear jump all over his mother playfully.

Gabe sighed. "I don't think that would work."

"B-but there has to be something we could do," Charlie said. "We can't leave them. He can't survive without his mama."

Gabe leaned his head back until his neck cracked, releasing some of the tension building in his shoulders.

"I don't know what you want me to do. Neither of us are veterinarians."

Charlie scratched the back of his neck then turned to Gabe with wide eyes. "No, but we are friends with a witch. Maybe she could help us. Maybe she has a spell or an... " Charlie's eyes became as big as saucers. "Or an herb."

Charlie tossed their sack onto the ground and dug through it, till he found the healing herbs. "If I give these to the mama, then she'll be okay, and then they'll both be okay."

Gabe was conflicted. If they gave the herbs to the bear, they wouldn't have any left for themselves if they got into a dangerous situation. But, if he didn't let Charlie give the bear the herbs, they would never leave the woods and thus, never become vampires. They probably wouldn't need the herbs anyways. They only had two items left, and Japan was a pretty safe country.

"Okay, you can give the bear the herbs—"

"Yes!" Charlie said as he jumped with the bag of herbs held high in the air.

"But you must run away as soon as she starts to heal. If you don't, we won't make it to the next ingredient, okay?"

Charlie nodded. "Definitely. I'm not dumb, Gabe. I know how protective mama bears can be. I've only watched like a hundred documentaries on them." Charlie skipped over to the mama bear and, like a dummy, placed his ear right next to her mouth. Yep, he placed his brain, his most valuable organ, right next to one of the most dangerous parts of a bear, their teeth.

Charlie gave him a thumbs up. "She's breathing, but it's very slow. I think we got here just in time."

Charlie pulled the herbs out of his bag, placed his hand under the bear's chin, and opened her mouth. Then he took the herbs and put them on her tongue and closed her mouth once more.

She didn't move for a few moments, then she used all her strength to swallow the herbs on her tongue. Her eyes opened, and a light shined from them before they returned to normal.

Charlie smiled, thankful it was working, before turning to the baby bear. "Now you have nothing to worry about." He reached out and patted the bear's head. He figured it would be his one and only chance to ever pet a real, live bear, and he wasn't going to give up the opportunity.

He turned back to the mama bear but frowned when he noticed her eyes start to droop again. Charlie placed his ear by the mama bear's mouth and listened. He waited and waited, but he heard nothing.

"She's not breathing!" Charlie shouted to Gabe. "The herbs aren't working." Charlie shook the mama bear's neck, trying to get her to react, but she didn't. She stayed still.

Gabe ran over and, against his better judgment, placed his own ear by the mama bear's mouth, hoping his friend had been mistaken. He hadn't been. The bear wasn't breathing.

A tear rolled down Charlie's cheek, but he quickly brushed it away. "She's gone," he whispered.

Gabe placed his hand on his friend's back. "I'm sorry, but at least you tried to help her. You did everything you could."

The baby bear pushed his head between Charlie's arms and looked up at him.

"What are we gonna do about him?" Charlie asked. "We can't leave him."

No, no, no, Gabe thought. There was no way they were bringing a bear along on their mission.

"Well, you said it yourself. He won't survive without his mama, so we couldn't help him," Gabe said. He felt like a jerk but better to be alive and annoying than dead.

Charlie looked back and forth between the mama and baby, then an idea came to him. "We could bring him with us, and if we're quick about our trip, we can bring him back through the portal with us and take him to a conservation place that helps orphaned bears."

It wasn't such a bad idea. They could save his life, make Charlie happy, and give him incentive to speed up their trip, so no more stops or unnecessary breaks. They would get home in no time.

"Fine, but if the calmness herbs start to wear off, we have to release him back into the wild. Deal?"

Charlie held his hand out. "Deal." They shook hands. Charlie scooped the baby bear into his arms and let the bear nuzzle his nose against his neck. Charlie placed his hand on the mama bear's neck and said, "I promise to make sure he's okay."

Charlie wiped another tear from his cheek and off they went, back to the trails.

Chapter 11: The Trade

The trail wasn't much of a trail.

It was tiny and covered in rocks, unlike the trails Gabe would walk with his mom by their library every Sunday afternoon. It took a while to get down the mountain.

Every so often Gabe would stop for a moment and look behind them at how far they'd gone. Each time he'd be surprised as to how high they had been at the start. They had arrived at the peak of the mountain, but Gabe tried not to think about it. He wasn't the biggest fan of heights.

He was thankful Charlie had been so prepared. He'd packed a couple pairs of water shoes, which were enough to keep the rocks out of their feet, and a jacket, so Charlie didn't look like some kid who woke up in the middle of the night and decided to go hiking. Sure, it was a strange combination, him wearing a baseball uniform with water shoes and Charlie wearing a jacket, pajama pants, and his own water shoes, but at least it was enough for people to only stare for a moment.

At the bottom of the trail was a flat, paved road. Charlie rubbed his knees and sat the bear down.

"Thank goodness we're at the bottom. Carrying Bearison did not make the hike any easier," Charlie said as he stretched his back.

"Well, you didn't have to carry him. He would've followed you—-wait, you named the bear?" Gabe asked with crossed arms.

Charlie smiled and scooped Bearison back into his arms. "Of course, I named him. We can't go around calling him the bear. It seems so impersonal." Charlie cleared his throat and pointed down the road. "Off we go."

Gabe worried his friend was getting a little too attached to the bear, but if it kept him happy and motivated, he wasn't going to complain.

They continued down the paved road, Gabe leading because he had the map. Gabe's stomach growled so often, Charlie could've closed his eyes and followed him by the sound. He hoped it didn't draw the attention of any animals nearby. He didn't know what they'd do if they came across another bear.

After about five minutes of walking, Charlie became bored. Since they no longer had to give their concentration to making it down the mountain, he started to grow agitated with the silence.

He stood up straight and started marching with a stern look on his face. He cleared his throat and said, "I don't know, but I've been told."

Gabe kept his eyes glued to the map. He was terrified the minute he took his eyes away he would miss a turn and lengthen their trip. Charlie kicked his shin.

"Dude, you're supposed to copy me. Come on, I don't know, but I've been told," Charlie nudged his head to Gabe since his arms were full of bear and waited for him to continue. Gabe stayed silent.

"Gaaaaabe," Charlie wined, "You're taking all the fun out of our quest."

Gabe was about to yell this wasn't some silly quest, and he didn't care if they had any fun. He just wanted to get home, but that wasn't fair to Charlie. He'd been the one to offer Gabe this opportunity, so he figured he could give in a little as long as it didn't slow down their trip.

"I don't know, but I've been told," Gabe said.

"I am never getting old," Charlie said.

"I am never getting old."

"No grey hair upon my head."

"No grey hair upon my head," Gabe repeated with a smirk.

"No aches and pains when I climb out of bed."

Gabe giggled. "No aches and pains when I climb out of bed."

"Sound off."

"Three, four," Gabe said through his laughter. He felt as if his chest grew a little lighter. Like someone removed a block from the tower collapsed on his lungs, making it a little easier to breathe. Maybe Charlie had the right idea. Maybe they could make this trip a little more fun.

They played a few rounds of eye spy, but by the time Gabe made a few guesses, Charlie had forgotten what it was he'd picked. They moved on to repeating each other's silly walks. Charlie did a one-legged jump that looked like he was playing hopscotch and Gabe copied him. Gabe did the weird sideways run he did in warmups at baseball practice, and Charlie tried to copy. After a few steps, one of his legs caught the other, and he tripped. On his way down he was able to turn over and let his side catch most of the damage to protect Bearison.

"You gotta put the bear down," Gabe said as he held out his hand to help Charlie stand.

"Only if you call him by his name," Charlie said as he got to his feet.

Gabe stared at the bear. He had big eyes and a long snout. Gabe tried to focus on these cute features and not the long claws. "Fine, put Bearison down," he said through gritted teeth.

Charlie placed his palm on the pavement.

"What are you doing?" Gabe asked.

"Making sure it's not too hot for him to walk on," Charlie said, keeping his palm pressed to the ground.

"It's like sixty degrees outside, and he's a freaking bear, Charlie." Gabe was seconds away from leaving his friend behind. "Put him down so we can go."

Once Charlie was satisfied that Bearison would be okay, he placed the bear on the ground. "There, if you get tired tell me, okay?" Charlie said as he patted Bearison's head. Bearison rubbed his nose against Charlie's leg. Charlie looked up at Gabe with a look of disgust. "You don't think he thinks I'm his new mom, do you?"

Gabe shook his head. "No, but you're gonna wish he did if his calming herbs wear off."

They continued down the road. Charlie glanced behind them every few seconds to make sure Bearison was okay.

Right as they reached the next turn in their map, Charlie punched Gabe.

"You don't have to hit me to get my attention. My ears work just fine," Gabe said as he looked up and glared. His glare faded into amazement as he saw what Charlie was pointing at.

Right in front of them, was a tall, wide mountain that dipped in the middle. From that dip rushed a thin river of water that became wider as the mountain split until it came to the edge and ran into a wide yet shallow lake below, creating a waterfall.

"That looks like the world's coolest waterslide," Charlie said as he stared with his mouth open.

"Yeah, more like the world's deadliest waterslide," Gabe said, looking at the large rocks at the bottom.

Charlie grabbed Gabe's arm and pulled him towards it. "Come on! Let's take a little break."

No, no, no. They didn't have time for a break. They had to get to the next item.

"But Charlie, what about Bearison? He needs to get to a conservation place soon," Gabe said while kneeling beside the bear.

Charlie glanced at the waterfall, then at Bearison. "But, but I," he stopped himself and frowned. "You're right."

He continued down the street, his hands in his pockets and his eyes cast to the ground. At first, the silence was relaxing, but Gabe would rather his friend be happily obnoxious than silently upset.

"Hey, Charlie, can you tell me a fun fact about bears?" Gabe asked. If there was one thing that could make his friend talk, it was discussing animals.

Charlie continued to stare at the ground. "They can run faster than a car," he mumbled.

"Wow," Gabe said, "that's pretty cool."

Charlie smirked. "Yeah, and they're like, so strong they can rip a car door off, so you wouldn't even be safe driving away."

Gabe didn't know why these facts made his best friend smile. All this information did for him was make him never want to drive anywhere near any forest or woods.

"And how many people get killed by bears per year?" Gabe asked. He didn't want to know, but Charlie's smile had returned, and he had more of a bounce to his step, so Gabe could deal with a few more terrifying facts.

"Like, only a couple people per year. You know what kills more people? Hotdogs."

The next few hours were filled with various facts about every animal Charlie could think of.

"Hey, did you know snails can sleep for up to three years?" Charlie asked as they crossed a bridge with a red, metal guard to keep them from falling into the river.

"Did you know that there is a type of jellyfish that is immortal?"

"Did you know that flamingos eat with their head upside down? It's because of the way their mouths are shaped and their weird necks."

"Did you know that lionesses do most of the hunting? Guess what the lions do," Charlie said.

"What?" Gabe asked.

"They are just lyin' around," Charlie answered then snorted.

Gabe laughed. He had to admit, these facts did make the trip go a lot faster. The scenery grew boring after a while. Even the river, which at the beginning of their trip had captured his attention with the tiny whitecaps the water made when it hit against the rocks, became boring and repetitive. All they saw was the river, trees, and a few identical bridges.

Eventually, they came to some farmland, but it wasn't much different than the farms they had around their house. There were green fields spread for miles. On those fields were older houses and sheds.

The cars were oddly shaped. They looked like someone took a van and squished it to make it thinner. Or maybe Gabe was seeing things. His head felt light, and his sight was blurry. The pain in his stomach had turned into nausea and every step felt heavier than the last. Like someone had dipped his feet in concrete and now he was dragging it around.

He was so focused on his map and the pain in his stomach, he didn't notice the large rock on the road ahead of him, and he tripped. "Agh," he said when he hit his arm against the ground.

"You gotta watch where you're going," Charlie said as he reached his hand out. Gabe got up, but as soon as he was upright, his vision grew black and he swayed to the side.

Charlie threw his arm around Gabe and kept him from tripping again. "Dude, are you okay?"

Gabe nodded with his eyes closed. When he opened them, his eyesight was back to normal. "Yeah, I just need to eat something."

"Well, it looks like you'll get your wish," Charlie said as he pointed to the town in front of them.

The town was small. It sat on the coast of a large river. There were many small buildings, but one, in particular, caught his eye, because in the window were pictures of food. Fish and soup and rice. Every picture made his stomach growl more and more.

"Let's go," Gabe said as he developed a second wind of energy, enough to get him inside the restaurant. The beautiful, delicious, gift from above restaurant was only a few steps away. He could make it. He just needed to get to the other side of those glass doors.

He made his way across the street to the tiny building, but right as he reached out to grab the handle, Charlie took his hand and pulled him away.

"Hey!" Gabe shouted as he yanked his hand away, "What was that for?"

"We have one tiny problem," Charlie said as he held up his fingers as though he was holding an invisible pencil.

"What now?" If this was about Bearison not being able to go into the restaurant, Gabe was going to scream.

"We don't have any money."

Crap, he was right. Gabe almost passed out. His mouth tried to water as he thought of the rice and fish and soup that were only a few feet away, but it was so dry from not drinking anything. He held his stomach and slid down the wall of the restaurant. He was so desperate that even the trashcan beside them smelled okay.

Charlie sat beside him and dug through their bag. "Ah-ha!" he said as he found what he was looking for.

Gabe looked over and with hopeful eyes asked, "Did you find food?"

Charlie shook his head. "Even better," he said as he pulled out his Nintendo.

Gabe smashed his teeth together. "How is your Nintendo better than food? What are we going to do? Eat the buttons?"

Gabe didn't know if he started shaking because of the rage or low blood sugar. Probably both. He tried to watch Charlie play his game as a distraction while he rested his feet, but all the movement on the screen made him even more nauseous. He looked off to the side where the river crashed on the rock-covered coast. There had to be a way they could get a few dollars or whatever kind of money they used in Japan. Maybe they could clean the restaurant? Maybe they could deliver a few meals around the small town? Maybe they could teach Bearison to do a few tricks and become street performers?

Just as his eyes started to grow weak, a girl and two boys, around seven or eight, came running up to them from a bike rack nearby. Charlie hid Bearison, who was thankfully asleep, behind Gabe, before they could get too close. Luckily, their eyes were more focused on Charlie's Nintendo.

"Nanishiteruno??" the first kid, a girl, asked.

"Miru koto ga dekimasu ka??" the shorter boy asked as they crowded around him.

They all gave Charlie pleading looks, but Charlie glanced between them confused.

"Uhh, I'm sorry. I don't speak a lot of Japanese... Uh." He hit his forehead, "Think Charlie, think. Okay, um, Anata wa watashi no ⌣ ga suki Nintendo?"

The kids nodded, causing Charlie's shoulders to relax. He turned to Gabe and whispered, "They wanna watch me play my game." He turned back to the kids. "Uh, hai."

The kids sat beside him and watched with amazement as Charlie zoomed through each level. They continued to watch until an older couple, came up to them and started speaking in Japanese. The kids frowned but didn't protest as they got up to follow their parents into the restaurant. The tallest boy stayed for a moment, before pointing to the Nintendo.

"Torēdo?" the boy asked as he pointed to the bike rack where three small bikes sat.

Charlie glanced at the bike and then back at the boy. "Uh, I'm sorry I don't know what you want."

The boy ran his tongue along his teeth and looked up at the sky then said, "I get Nintendo, you get jitensha," he said as he pointed to the bike.

Charlie's eyes widen. "Oh, you wanna trade my Nintendo for your bike. No, thank you," he said while shaking his head.

The boy frowned and stuck his hands in his pocket. He pulled out a wad of bills and flipped through them, holding out all ten. "You get yen. I get Nintendo?"

Gabe's stared at the boy who was holding ten thousand yen. He didn't know what that equated to in American dollars, but he knew that would more than cover a meal in the restaurant.

"Do it, Charlie, then we can eat. If we don't, we won't make it the rest of the way," Gabe pleaded. His stomach hurt so bad he couldn't sit up straight.

Charlie looked back and forth between the boy and Gabe. He then looked at his Nintendo and back at Gabe.

Gabe knew this was a big decision for Charlie. He'd had that Nintendo for years, and they'd played a lot of games on it together. He took it with him everywhere he went. Once, when he was asked if he'd give up his Nintendo to save his father's life, he hesitated before saying yes uncertainly.

Charlie took one more glance at Gabe, the Nintendo, and the boy, then said, "Fine, you get Nintendo. I get yen and bike," he said as he pointed to the bike rack.

This must've been quite the deal for the boy because he ran to his bike and pedaled it over so fast, he almost lost balance and fell.

He handed the bike and the yen to Charlie and held out his hands. Charlie held the Nintendo against his chest as though giving it a hug before holding it out to the boy.

"Here," he said with a shaky voice, "I hope it brings you as much joy as it brought me."

The boy tilted his head. He didn't understand anything Charlie had said, but he smiled and waved as he ran into the restaurant.

Gabe's legs wobbled as he stood and walked over to Charlie, who was placing the bike against the side of the restaurant. Gabe put his hand on Charlie's shoulder and said, "I know that was hard for you."

Charlie shrugged him off and shook his head. "Let's just go eat." They used the bike and the trashcan to make a barrier for Bearison then went back to the glass doors.

As soon as they walked into the restaurant, Charlie's eyes went to the boy who was playing his Nintendo at one of the tables. Gabe pushed Charlie to the counter, knowing he'd stand there and stare until the family left if he had the choice.

The man at the counter only spoke Japanese, so Gabe pointed to the picture of the fish and rice on the window and then held up two fingers. He gave the man some of their yen then went to a table and waited for their food to be ready.

A few minutes passed before a tall, slim man walked into the restaurant. He ordered something in Japanese, but his accent was strange, different than the man at the counters or the children they'd spoken to. It was more like Charlie's when he spoke in Japanese.

The man sat at the table beside them, giving Charlie an odd look before he pulled out his phone. Gabe didn't blame him. Charlie had turned back to the family and was continuing to watch the boy play his Nintendo.

"Charlie," Gabe said, "stop staring. It's weird. I know you miss your Nintendo, but watching will only make it worse."

Charlie turned to face him and sighed. "You're right."

The tall man beside them sat his phone on the table and leaned over to them. "Are you two from America?" he asked.

The boys looked at each other with wide eyes then nodded. "Yeah," Charlie said, "we're on vacation."

"With our parents," Gabe lied, not wanting to let a stranger know they were by themselves without any adults.

"Cool, me too. Well, I'm not on vacation. I live here," he said.

"Really?" Charlie asked, "How? I've always wanted to live here."

"I'm an English as a second language teacher, so I have a work visa," he explained.

Charlie placed his elbow on the table and rested his head against his hand, staring in awe. Teaching and Japan were two of his favorite things. "That sounds awesome."

"You should look into it when you're older," the man said as his order was called. "Well, it was nice talking to you." He stood and went over to the counter, leaving them alone again.

"Isn't that awesome? I could live here. I could see everything. The ice festival, Tokyo, older traditional Japanese homes, all the beautiful sights—"

"Except, you're not going to be able to become a teacher because I don't think they hire thirteen-year-olds," Gabe said.

Charlie rolled his eyes. "Yeah, I wasn't planning on applying right now, but in a few years, I'll"—he frowned—"still be thirteen."

Charlie looked at his hands and counted his fingers, something he always did when he was upset. Gabe didn't like bringing Charlie down, but he didn't want to lie either. He wanted his friend to know the decision he was about to make was life changing.

Gabe got his food and scarfed it into his mouth. He looked disgusting and any other time Gabe would be polite and respectful, but he hadn't eaten in almost twenty-four hours. His stomach felt as though it was about to cave in on itself.

With every scoop of rice, he became more and more relaxed, like all the little things that had been annoying him didn't matter anymore. He could go another few hours walking and listen to more interesting animal facts.

Charlie's mind seemed to be wandering since he was taking longer to eat. He stared into his bowl of rice and moved his fork around, taking a small bite.

"I don't want to rush you, but we should go. If we're lucky we can get the other two ingredients by nightfall," said Gabe as he wiped his mouth.

Charlie ate a few more bites then said, "I'm done."

Gabe's jaw dropped when he saw Charlie's not finished plate. He pulled Charlie's bowl towards him and gobbled the rest of the fish and rice into his mouth. It was so good, he could've eaten ten bowls.

They left the restaurant and went back to Bearison, who was awake and lying on his back, moving his legs around as though he was running. His tongue was laying out of his mouth, down the side of his face, and resting on the gravel.

"Aww," Charlie said as he moved the bike and scooped the bear into his arms. He placed Bearison in the bike's basket and smiled. "At least this will help us get to our next ingredient faster. Now, who's gonna ride the handlebars?"

Chapter 12: The Monster

Riding on the handlebars was not as fun as it looked in movies, Gabe thought as he held on for dear life, especially when you had a bear resting its head on your knee. Every time he looked down at Bearison, he pictured the calming herbs wearing off and him turning around and attacking Gabe's leg while he had nowhere to go.

Charlie was a good rider, but he was in a new country and had to look around Gabe to see where he was going, so he swerved a lot. They almost hit three cars and were close to tumbling into the river a time or two, but they made it a good way before Bearison started to whine.

Charlie skidded to a stop and held the bike as Gabe slid off. Gabe hit his knees and placed his palms on the ground, thankful they were still alive.

Charlie lifted Bearison out of his basket and placed him on the ground, kneeling beside him. "What's wrong, buddy?"

Bearison walked around the gravel a bit before leaning down and peeing.

Gabe took a few deep breaths to get his heart rate under control. He looked around at the new town they'd ended up in then said, "Charlie, look."

Charlie looked to where Gabe was staring and saw a bus station. "No way, you don't think they have a bus to where we're going, do you?"

Gabe stood. "Only one way to find out."

Gabe decided to stay outside with Bearison while Charlie went into the station. He didn't want to be the babysitter or bear-sitter, but Charlie knew a few words in Japanese, so he won.

Gabe kept Bearison in the basket, even when he whined and looked up at Gabe with his big, brown eyes.

"That doesn't work on me," he said as Bearison placed his paws on the basket's lip and put his head on top. Gabe glared. "Stop."

Bearison tilted his head and opened his eyes so wide, Gabe was worried they might pop out. Darn it! Why did baby animals have to be so cute?

"Ugh, fine." He scooped Bearison out of the basket and placed him on the ground, letting him walk around. The bear walked right on top of Gabe's feet and plopped his belly onto his water shoes.

"Seriously?" he asked the bear as though he would answer. He shoved his hands into his pocket and stared at the sky, praying Charlie would hurry up.

A few minutes later, Charlie exited the bus station, waving two tickets in the air.

"I got em. It'll take us two buses to get there, but it will be much faster than taking the bike," Charlie said as he placed his sack on the ground.

"Also less deadly," Gabe muttered under his breath.

"What?" Charlie asked.

"Nothing."

Charlie unzipped his sack then rubbed the top of Bearison's head. "This will be for a short bit, okay? This will help us get you to your new home faster." Charlie lifted the limp, half-asleep bear and placed him into the bag. He then zipped the bag most of the way shut, leaving it open enough to make sure Bearison had sufficient oxygen. "They don't allow dogs on trains," Charlie explained as he put the sack's strap over his shoulder. "I don't think they'd make an exception for a bear."

They only had to wait a few moments before loading onto the bus. The bus was packed, so they had to sit by the front in the sideways seat that looked like a small couch with thin, dark pink cushions. Charlie slid their sack under their chair while Gabe pushed himself into the seat's corner and closed his eyes. Though the seats were thin and hard, they beat riding metal handlebars.

He drifted to sleep as the bus took off.

In his dream, he was walking down the street, but something about it was off. He was by a busy intersection, but there were no stop lights, only metal poles with yellow, blinking dots. How would the cars know when to stop and go? Gabe thought. That's when he noticed there was no one driving the cars. The passengers sat in the back seats, playing games, and watching TV while the front was covered in wires and blinking lights. The cars blinked their lights at each other when they reached the stop, and whoever blinked their lights twice in a row went next.

This must be the future. He looked around in awe and wondered how far ahead he was. What else could be different? Maybe they had robot dogs. Maybe they had food that could keep you full for a week. Maybe they had a cure for schizophrenia.

He strolled down the sidewalk and glanced around at all the stores. It reminded him of the time his family took a trip to New York City. There were plenty of tall, professional buildings that always bored Gabe, but there were also heavily detailed historical buildings. He passed a library with a stone statue zoo out front. Every animal he could think of and more were carved around the stairs, ramps, and doorways. They had a giraffe standing next to the building, with its head resting on the library as though it were a pillow. He was about to go inside this fantastic building when a man placed a hand on his's shoulder.

"Hey, kid," he said with a frown. "Shouldn't you be in school?"

Gabe looked around, trying to figure out what year he was in. He only had five more years of public school left, and he knew he was more than five years in the future.

"No," Gabe said, turning back to the library. He tried again to take a step towards the entrance when the man grabbed his arm.

"I think your parents need to be given a call and told their child is out roaming around in the city by themselves," the man said while pulling out his cellphone.

Gabe tried to yank his arm away as his heart raced in his chest. He couldn't let the man call his dad. If he did, his dad would have to take off work to come get him and then he would be even more stressed.

But then Gabe realized something. He was in the future. Were his parents still alive? Were they gone? Did he have to watch them... go?

"Um, excuse me, sir," Gabe said as he stopped trying to pull his arm away. "What year is it?"

The man grew concerned. "It's twenty-one forty-eight, son. Are you okay?"

Gabe started to hyperventilate. If it was twenty-one forty-eight, then he was over a hundred years old, meaning his parents were probably... Well, he didn't even want to think about it.

He slipped his thin arm out of the man's grasp and took off down the sidewalk. He only got a few buildings down when a middle-aged man came running up to him, pointing at him accusingly.

"You! Come here you little brat!" the man shouted. Gabe froze and turned back to the first man, who was coming at him from the other side of the sidewalk. He had nowhere to go but across the street, where cars were zooming by. Every time he reached his foot out to take a step, he'd have to pull it back as another car rushed by, creating a small gust of wind.

The men were both a few feet from him. "You better stay right there," the second man shouted while waving his finger.

The first man stopped to take a few breaths. "What's going on?" he asked the second man.

"This kid has been running away from our home almost every single day."

"Oh, are you his father?" the first man asked, his hands on his knees.

The second man laughed. *"Kid's got no parents. He's in my group home. We take in runways, and this kid tops the list."*

Runaways? What would he have to run away from? He was over a hundred years old; he could take care of himself.

He turned back around to the first man, and that's when he caught his reflection in the glass of a store. He still looked the same as he had over a hundred years before. He must've succeeded in becoming a vampire. No wonder they were all after him. They thought he was some random kid.

He tried to think of a way to explain everything to the men, without telling them he was a vampire when a woman in her forties ran across the street with a hand over her mouth. With every step, a white circle emitted from her foot, creating her own personal crosswalk. The cars stopped and waited for her to cross.

Gabe didn't have much time to think about how cool that was because the woman got only halfway across the street before saying, *"I know you. We were in a group home together for a couple of months thirty years ago."* She looked him up and down, frighted. *"You haven't aged a day."*

Oh, no, this was not good.

She pointed to him and whispered, *"Monster."*

The men also pointed their fingers at him and said much louder, "Monster. This kid's a monster."

Everyone on the street turned and stared. "Monster, he's a monster! Destroy the monster!" they shouted.

He had nowhere to go, nowhere to turn. He was surrounded. He backed up until his back hit the glass store behind him. He curled into a ball as the crowd grew closer.

"Monster, monster, monster!" they shouted in unison.

He closed his eyes and put his arms by his head, squeezing them tightly against his ears, but he could still hear their shouts. He wanted to go home to his family. He wanted to be safe. He wanted to be held by his mother, wanted to be protected by his father. He didn't want to be a monster. He just wanted to go home.

Chapter 13: The Material Boys

He was awoken by Charlie hitting him with a shoe.

"Dude, wake up," Charlie whispered. "You're having a bad dream."

Gabe opened his eyes and looked around the bus. Two people were staring at him, which made him uneasy, but as soon as they noticed he noticed they were staring, they turned back to their phones.

"Are you okay?" Charlie asked.

Gabe sat up straight, his back cracking multiple times as it released the pressure of leaning over for hours. "I don't know," he answered. His heart was still pumping fast from the fear though it was coming back down to a normal pace as he realized it was all a dream. His parents were still alive, and no one was pointing at him or calling him a monster.

But just because it wasn't real, didn't mean it couldn't happen one day. If they went through with becoming vampires, he would have to outlive his parents. He guessed most kids did that anyway, but they were supposed to be old themselves. You weren't

supposed to lose your parents when you were a kid.
You weren't supposed to live for an eternity. It goes
against the rules of nature, and Gabe was one to
always follow the rules.

Before the dream, the thought of living forever
always sounded fun. He'd be able to see all the future
technology, he'd be able to have any job he ever
wanted, and he'd be able to waste a ton of time lying
around, watching TV, because he had all the time in
the world. But that wouldn't be true for them. They
would be thirteen forever. Thirteen was not the best
age. Sure, there are sports and video games and field
trips, but there's also homework, and curfews, and you
couldn't go anywhere or do anything without an adult
saying it was okay. That was fine with Gabe since he
was supposed to grow up, but turning into a vampire
would change that. He would have to live under the
rules of the adults forever. Could he do that?

Charlie guided Gabe off their first bus and onto
the second while Gabe stayed deep in thought. He
started to grow unsure of their decision. Maybe they
were making a mistake. Maybe they needed to think
things through a little more, but how could he suggest
that to Charlie?

Gabe stared at the bus's front windshield for the
entire duration of the ride. He didn't say a word to
Charlie, who was too focused on Bearison to notice.

Images from his dream kept swirling around in his
head, making him doubt what they were doing. Maybe
he should've thought about it a little more. He
should've written a pro/con list before he decided to go
on this quest. He loved pro/con lists. Pro, becoming a

vampire meant he could help protect his mom; con, he'd live forever. Pro, Charlie wouldn't be mad at him for changing his mind halfway through their mission, and con, people might see him as a monster. Pro, he'd be better at baseball, but con, he didn't care to be better at baseball because he didn't even like playing. He wanted so badly to find the right answer. He needed a sign he was making the right decision. Something that would show him he wasn't about to ruin his life.

Before he knew it, they arrived at the bus station.

After being on the tip of a mountain in the middle of nowhere, arriving in a city was quite the shock. There were huge, grey, tan, and red brick buildings surrounding them on all sides. Most of the buildings had signs with Japanese writing on top and English on the bottom, but the thing that made it the most different from the cities back home were the mountains in the distance.

"Huh," Charlie said as he read the map with narrowed eyebrows.

Gabe leaned over to see what was confusing his friend when he saw the map was now gone, and in its place were the words, Await Further Instructions.

"What's that supposed to mean?" Gabe asked, frustrated. Then he realized, maybe this was a sign. Maybe all the challenges they've had to face, all the blocks in their path, were there to stop them from making a horrible mistake.

"I don't know," Charlie said as he rolled the map up, "But I guess we have to wait for the next map. I'm sure there's something we can do around here to pass the time."

Good, that meant Gabe would have more time to figure out how to tell Charlie he was unsure about their decision. Maybe taking his mind off the mission for a while was just what he needed.

They walked down the street, passing building after building, looking for something to entertain them. Gabe felt as though he was in a parallel world because the buildings were like ones in the city close to where he lived, but they had Japanese writing on the signs. Most of the cars that drove past them were like the ones they'd seen on their walk, almost identical to the ones in America, but squashed so thin they could have a six-lane street instead of four. Gabe sighed in relief when he saw the stop lights were identical to the ones back home and not futuristic like in his dream.

"Hey, look, a mall," Charlie said as he pointed to a large building. Charlie was about to go towards it when Gabe grabbed his arm.

"Don't you think it's a little suspicious to walk into a store with a large sack?" he asked.

Charlie glanced at his sack, which was so long Bearison had been able to walk back and forth through it during their bus rides, causing a few passengers to stare.

"Well, we can't leave him out here. Oh, I could go buy him a sweatshirt, and then we could walk him inside like he's a dog," Charlie said as he placed the sack on the ground and turned to go inside.

"Except," Gabe said, making Charlie freeze, "you don't have any money."

They had spent the rest of the money from selling Charlie's Nintendo on the bus tickets. Charlie's head hit his chest.

"So, now I don't have a Nintendo or enough money to buy my bear a sweatshirt. What do I have?" He shook his head then unzipped the sack. "Maybe I packed an extra sweatshirt or t-shirt or something." He checked every inch of the bag. He even held up Bearison and checked under him, but all he had were a couple dead flashlights. As a last resort, he unzipped the side pocket and glanced inside.

"Uh, Gabe, you're never gonna guess what I found," Charlie said as he kept his eyes on the treasure in the side pocket.

Gabe rolled his eyes and glanced inside. Knowing Charlie, it was probably a Nintendo game or half a slice of pizza.

It was neither. The pocket was mostly empty, besides one, tiny, black credit card.

"Woah," Gabe said.

"Wait," Charlie said, his shoulders tense. "We had this the entire time? I didn't have to sell my Nintendo?" He punched his knee.

"Well, it's your parents' card. It's not like we can use it," said Gabe.

"Why not?" Charlie asked as he slid it out and flipped it over again and again as though making sure it was real.

Was he crazy? Was he really asking why?

"Uh, maybe because it's your parent's hard-earned money and not yours, so that's stealing," Gabe said. Surely Charlie wasn't actually debating using his parent's credit card. Breaking a few necessary rules to get them to become vampires Gabe could deal with, it was all a means to an end, but taking money from Charlie's parents? That was just wrong.

"Gabe, Gabe, Gabe. You don't understand because you have a nice, sweet little family. You spend time together, support each other. Your dad, he shows up to all your baseball games, right?" Gabe nodded, unsure what that had to do with stealing. "Well, my dad never shows up to my gymnastics competitions. He says he's busy with work, blah blah blah, then he buys me something, so I'll forgive him. It's our system. Your parents support you; mine buy my love."

Gabe had to admit, Charlie had a point. Gabe's dad worked two jobs, yet he was somehow always there when Gabe needed him. Charlie's parents spent family suppers on the phone, never came to his school family nights, and always seemed annoyed when Gabe slept over. But even then, stealing was wrong. You couldn't steal from people just because they were rude. He decided he'd use the tactic his Mama always used on him when he was making the wrong decision.

"Fine, but know that what you decide will follow you for the rest of your life. The decision you make will show what kind of a man you are," Gabe said, sure this would deter Charlie from making the wrong decision.

Charlie shrugged. "Okay, wait here while I go buy Bearison a sweatshirt." Charlie jumped to his feet and skipped to the mall while Gabe watched in amazement.

Huh, maybe that only worked on him.

Charlie ran out a few moments later with a bright pink sweatshirt. He gently guided Bearison's arms through the arm holes and covered his bottom with the edge of the sweatshirt. When he was done, he held out his arms, proud of his work.

"Tada, now, he looks like one adorable dog."

Gabe followed Charlie into the mall. He figured he couldn't stop Charlie from making bad choices, but he didn't have to make them himself. He also figured there was no harm in looking around.

The mall was huge. It was twice as tall as the malls he'd been to. There were four stories, and the roof was a long, glass dome that brought in the setting September sun. Gabe took a deep breath, drawing in the aroma from the first floor. They were surrounded by multiple restaurants squeezed right next to each other in tiny spaces. In the middle of the room sat groups of tables for the diners.

Gabe's stomach growled. Apparently, the rice and fish, though filling at the time, were not enough to hold him over till the end of their trip.

No, they had to because Gabe was not going to spend a dime of Charlie's parents' money.

Charlie pointed to one of the shops. A candy shop. Gabe sighed. This was going to be harder than he thought.

Charlie walked to the shop with Bearison on his tail, plopping his paws along as though he were tap dancing. Gabe slumped his shoulders and followed. The inside of the shop was even more impressive than the outside. It made Gabe's mouth water. There were gummies of all shapes, both sour and sweet. There were hard candies and sugar in different colors and chocolate. They had chocolate-covered everything. Raisins, peanuts, coffee beans. You could get as much as you wanted because the candy came out of long tubes and small, plastic boxes you could scoop from.

"This is gonna be awesome," Charlie said as he grabbed a couple empty bags. He ran around to every tube that had anything of interest and let the bag fill to the brim. He had bags of all kinds of sour gummies, from gummy worms to gummy bears. He had hard candy pieces, gumballs, and Smarties. When he got to the end of the gummy line, where the chocolate was placed, Gabe was sure his friend was done. Charlie hated chocolate. He said it didn't have enough flavor. Gabe figured all the sour candy had destroyed Charlie's tastebuds.

But Charlie didn't stop when he got to the chocolate. He grabbed a few candy bars, some chocolate-covered raisins, and a chocolate-shaped wand.

"I didn't know you started liking chocolate," Gabe said as he followed Charlie to the checkout counter.

Charlie looked everywhere but Gabe. "Uh, yeah," he said nervously, "I wanted to give it another try. Just like you always say, our tastebuds change all the time."

Charlie grabbed the candy off the counter and darted to the food court, not looking back at Gabe or even Bearison until they got to a table and sat. Charlie took a handful of sour gummies and popped them into his mouth, moaning with delight. His goofy smile made Gabe smile. Then he realized, this was it. Charlie was happy, so this was the perfect time to tell him his doubts about the mission.

But then Charlie sat the bag of gummies on the table and picked the bag of chocolate up off his lap. He frowned as he ripped open the candy bar and stared at the chocolate in disgust. He glanced over at Gabe, then back at the bar, and took the tiniest bite off the corner. Though he looked like he wanted to spit it out, he chewed and swallowed the chocolate then shook his head.

"You know what," Charlie said as he placed the chocolate bar on a napkin. "I still don't like chocolate. You can have it."

Gabe stared at the bar on the table, his mouth watered so much he had to swallow multiple times. He grabbed the bar, ripped the corner open, and bit half the bar into his mouth.

Charlie smiled a proud smile and took another bite of his gummy candy. Gabe had no idea what he had to be proud about, besides trying chocolate, though it wasn't exactly a vegetable.

"Here," Charlie said as he held the bag filled with the rest of the chocolate out to Gabe. "You can have this too."

Gabe grabbed the bag so fast you could barely see his hand. He gobbled up the chocolate bar, threw handfuls of chocolate-covered raisins into his mouth, and licked every spec off his fingers. It was the most delicious chocolate he'd ever had.

His stomach felt heavy, a little pained from all the junk, but his head felt clear, and for the first time since he'd run away, he was able to sit back and take a moment to relax.

"Come on. Let's go check out some shoes," Charlie said as he stood.

Gabe groaned. He wanted to sit until they received their next map. Maybe in that time, he'd be able to gather the confidence to tell Charlie about his doubts.

He followed Charlie to the shoe store. It was not like the shoe stores Gabe was used to. You know, the type of store you go to when your second cousin got a hole in his tennis shoes, so he couldn't hand them down, so your parents had to take you to the shoe store with the half-off stickers that still made them wince when they saw the prices.

No, this store was the kind you walked right past. They were over-priced, flashy, and had little logos that showed people you had money. Why anyone would spend that kind of money on a pair of shoes was beyond Gabe, and yet, he would do anything for just one pair.

He followed Charlie around as he picked up shoe after shoe, looking them over from every angle. Each time he squeezed or pulled at one, Gabe cringed. He couldn't imagine handling expensive shoes like that.

Finally, Charlie picked up a tan pair with dark brown stripes, which surprised Gabe. He figured Charlie would go for the bright red or green, something that screams 'look at me', but these were more subtle, almost like you could wear them to church and people might think they were dress shoes.

Charlie paid for the shoes then headed to the mall hallway and sat on one of the benches. He slid off his water shoes and unstrapped the high-tops, but they couldn't get past his heel.

"Oh, no," Charlie said while shaking his head, "I got the wrong size."

"You can return them," Gabe said as he wrestled with Bearison over Charlie's water shoe.

Charlie opened his mouth to respond, but nothing came out. He glanced at the store's window, then at the shoes, then back at the window. He balled his hand into a fist and swung his arm against his chest.

"I would, but I don't think I know enough Japanese for them to understand what I'm saying. Here, why don't you try them on?" Charlie asked as he held the shoe out.

Gabe stared at the shoe as though it were a beautiful painting stolen from a museum. Scratch that, Gabe never understood art, but he did see the beauty in the tan high top held out in front of him.

Don't get ahead of yourself, he thought. They probably won't even fit.

He took the shoe and unstrapped it. He pulled the top apart, then pushed his foot in. He had to slam the bottom against the ground a few times to press his heel in, but it fit perfectly.

"Amazing," Charlie said, but something about his tone seemed off to Gabe. Maybe he was upset his new shoes didn't fit?

Gabe stood and walked around, trying to form the shoe to his foot. It felt as though he were walking on air, like his feet were weightless.

"How do they feel?" Charlie asked.

Gabe froze. "Um, great, thank you."

Charlie hopped to his feet. "No, problem." He pointed down the hall. "To the next store."

Bearison padded along beside Gabe as he followed Charlie. Gabe felt a little safer in his thick, high-top shoes. They could protect him if Bearison started to attack, at least long enough to get away.

After they visited the next two stores, Gabe started growing worried about his friend's intelligence. At the clothing store, he accidentally bought two of each of the four t-shirts he wanted.

When Gabe asked him about it, he hit his forehead and said, "Oh, I saw a sign that said two for one, and I thought that meant you had to buy two of the same shirts."

Gabe had looked around the store but hadn't seen any sign that said anything about a sale. He guessed Charlie had read something in Japanese.

Then when they got to the sunglass store, Charlie grabbed a pair of sunglasses, leaned down to Bearison, then grabbed another pair of the same sunglasses. After paying for both pairs, Gabe asked him why he needed two pairs.

Charlie looked into the bag and laughed. "Oh, I must've gotten distracted by Bearison and forgotten I'd already picked up a pair. Silly me."

It wasn't until they got to the video game store, that Gabe became suspicious.

Charlie had pointed to the Nintendos behind the checkout man's head then held up two fingers. Gabe watched as the man scanned the Nintendos. The number doubled on the screen, so Charlie couldn't lie and say there was a sale. He couldn't believe he'd fallen for it. Charlie was trying to trick him into letting him buy things for him. He watched as Charlie slid the card into the machine then followed him back to the hall.

"So, accidentally read a sign wrong again?" Gabe asked with crossed arms. Did he want a Nintendo? Sure. Did he want Charlie's parents to pay for a Nintendo for him without their permission? No.

Charlie shook his head. "No, this is a birthday present for a relative."

Gabe frowned. Oh. Well, now he felt dumb, and a little disappointed, but why did he feel that way? He didn't even want the stupid Nintendo. The special edition that came preloaded with games. The one that was a cool, bright green instead of the normal colors. Gabe didn't want any of that.

They headed to a watch shop, the kind that didn't want thirteen-year-old boys looking around. Especially boys like Charlie who were prone to breaking things.

"Charlie, you're not really looking to buy a fancy watch, are you?" Gabe whispered as they looked through the glass cases.

"No, I always come to these kinds of stores with my dad, but he picks out the boring watches. I've always wanted to try on one of those that tell time in multiple countries, but he never let me," Charlie said as he continued to browse. He pointed to one with multiple faces and a dark blue strap.

The woman behind the counter didn't seem too keen on the idea of letting Charlie try on the watch, but she pulled the container from under the glass and lifted it out of the foam. She sat it on Charlie's thin wrist and clasped it. It dangled a bit, but Gabe had to admit, he looked cool, like a spy.

"Do you wanna try on one?" Charlie asked.

Gabe took a step back and shook his head. "No, it's fine."

"Dude, you're not doing anything wrong by trying on a watch. That's what you supposed to do."

He had a point. Besides, the store was empty, so they weren't making anyone wait.

He pointed to the watch beside the one Charlie had picked. It had a brown strap and a single face, but it called out to him. The woman slid it onto his wrist.

The watch made him feel taller, stronger, like a grown man. He felt like all he needed was a fancy suit and he could go into a business meeting, waving his finger around at all the people who worked for him, like he had the power to lead an entire company, just because of the fancy wristband that could tell time.

But then he remembered why this watch was so different than the others. It reminded him of his papa's watch. The watch he had promised to give to Gabe when he turned eighteen.

"The day you become a man, Hijo" is what he said to Gabe, pride shining in his eyes. The thought of Gabe becoming a strong, smart, powerful man meant everything to his papa.

But he wasn't going to be a man. He was going to be a kid forever. Would his papa still give him the watch? Would he still respect him like a man or treat him like a kid?

Gabe waited until the woman removed the watch from his hand before darting out of the store. He ran to one of the benches in the hall and placed his head in his hands. Don't cry, he thought. If I cry, Charlie will know something was wrong.

Maybe that would be a good thing, though? Maybe if Charlie asked him what was wrong, he could finally answer that he didn't know if he was ready to become a vampire, and he wanted to take some more time to think about it.

He wiped the tears from his eyes and looked around, trying to calm himself. That's when he saw his sign.

There was a mother, standing by the bench across from him, holding her small child in her arms. The child was cold, so the mother took off her own jacket and wrapped it around the child. He could tell the woman was tired by the way she rubbed her eyes then her swollen ankles, but she kept holding the child, kept rocking it until it calmed down.

It reminded him of the many, many times his mother had given him her snack, her water bottle, her jacket. She always gave him everything, even if it meant she would have to suffer. She was an angel, and she deserved to be treated as one. It was in that moment he realized there wasn't any decision to make.

He had to become a vampire.□

Chapter 14: The Second Ingredient

Charlie met Gabe at the bench. He didn't seem to notice Gabe had been crying, much to his relief. He placed his bags on the ground, leaned back, and asked, "Where should we go next?"

"Maybe we should check the map to see if it's changed," Gabe suggested. He didn't have a moment to waste. If he was going through with it, it needed to be as soon as possible, before he tried to talk himself out of it again.

Charlie frowned. "I don't think it's changed."

"Well, why don't we just check," Gabe said as he leaned down to grab the map Charlie had hidden under his pant leg, the bottom of which was shoved in his dirty sock. Charlie pulled his foot away.

"I just don't know why it would be any different than it was when we checked a few hours ago."

Gabe reached for the map again, this time grabbing it and unrolling it, holding it far away from Charlie. The words were gone, and in their place was a new, much shorter map.

"Ah-ha, I was right," Gabe said, smiling, but then he noticed Charlie's disappointment. "What's wrong? This is great. We're one step closer to getting all the ingredients."

"Yeah, that's great," Charlie said, but his voice said it was anything but good news.

"What's wrong?" Gabe asked, hoping his friend would give him a straight answer. He didn't have time to play guessing games; he had to get home.

"I thought we were having a great time together," Charlie admitted.

"Why would that make you sad then?" Gabe asked.

"Because I—never mind, let's go," Charlie said as he picked up his bags and walked to the exit of the mall.

Gabe glanced at Bearison, who tilted his head like he was saying, "I don't know why he's upset either."

He walked with Bearison out of the mall. Outside the exit, he saw Charlie unzipping the sack he'd placed by the door and stuffing all the shirts, sunglasses, and Nintendos inside aggressively. He threw the sack over his back and shoved his hands into his pockets.

The walk to the next ingredient only took about twenty minutes. Gabe didn't look up until the dot that represented where they were and the cross that represented their destination was right on top of each other. When he did, he was thankful to be face to face with a sign that was in both Japanese and English.

"Hokkaido University," Charlie read as he pointed his flashlight at the sign. Gabe was thankful Charlie had remembered to pick up some batteries at the

electronic store because they would be in complete
darkness without the flashlights.

Gabe checked the map. "Okay, we need to find a
ginkgo tree and get some leaves from it."

They continued to walk until they found four long
lines of identical trees lining two sidewalks with a road
in the middle. Gabe looked back and forth at the sketch
of the tree and then at the actual trees.

"This looks like it," he said. He pointed his
flashlight at the leaves. Most of them were green, but a
few of them had started turning yellow. "If we had
been here a couple weeks later, we'd be able to pick
some off the ground. What are we going to do now?"

"I'll climb the tree," Charlie said. He cracked his
knuckles, then his neck, and headed toward the closest
tree. "You be on lookout." He told Gabe as he wrapped
his arms around the tree, as though giving it a hug, and
tried to drag himself up. "Mmm," he groaned, then let
go and huffed. "Well, uh…"

He looked the tree up and down then started
hopping. "Oh, I got this," he said as he backed up. He
dug his toes into the ground then pushed off and ran at
the tree, jumping and attaching himself to its trunk. He
put his hand where the trunk split in two and tried to
pull himself up, but there was nothing else within his
reach to grab ahold of. He slipped to the ground and
fell on his butt.

Gabe placed the map in front of his face, so
Charlie wouldn't see him laugh. When he got all his
chuckles out, he looked back at the leaves and sighed.
"What now?"

Charlie got up and squatted with his hands held together. "Gabe, step on my hands, and I'll push you up."

"No," Gabe immediately replied.

Charlie stood tall and held his arms out. "Why not?"

"'Cause you're gonna drop me."

"Will not."

"Will too."

They stood with crossed arms, staring at each other, neither willing to back down. There had to be a way to get a leaf, without either one falling on the road and breaking their leg.

Maybe they could sneak into the school, pretending to be lost, Gabe thought. While Charlie distracts the janitor, Gabe would take his badge then sneak into the janitor's closet and grab his ladder, somehow getting it outside without looking suspicious, then—

"Come here, little guy. I got a treat for you," Charlie said as he held a gummy worm out in front of Bearison's nose. The bear took slow steps towards Charlie, staring at the gummy worm like it was hypnotizing him. Every step Bearison took forward, Charlie would take one backward until he was right next to one of the trees. He tossed the gummy bear onto a tree limb, and said, "Go get it, boy."

The bear dug his claws into the tree and pulled himself up, desperate to get the gummy. He walked out onto one of the thin limbs, where the gummy sat, taking slow, unsteady steps towards it. Charlie stood underneath him with his arms out, ready to catch him if he fell.

Gabe didn't understand what Charlie was trying to do until Bearison's weight shook the branch, making a few leaves fall off and float to the ground. Gabe grabbed a plastic bag from their sack and picked the leaves up while Bearison scooted himself backward and then slid down the tree.

Charlie gathered him into his arms and held him like a baby. "Good job, buddy. Tell him he did a good job, Gabe."

Gabe placed the bag into their sack. "He's a bear; he wouldn't understand what I was saying. I could say, you're a horrible bear and you like to eat poop, and he wouldn't care."

Charlie sharply inhaled and placed his hand over his mouth while his elbow held Bearison's stomach. "How could you say something like that. What would we have done without him? He saved our quest."

Gabe sighed. Fine, technically the bear did help them out. "Thank you," Gabe muttered as he clenched the map.

"Thank you, what?" Charlie said while pointing his ear towards Gabe.

Gabe looked to the sky. "Thank you... Bearison."

Charlie smiled and placed Bearison back on the ground. "Great, now, where to next?"

Gabe unrolled the map and groaned because written again were the words: Await further instructions.

"Seriously?" Gabe asked as he crumbled the map. "No, I'm not waiting any longer. Portal to her and ask her what's taking so long."

"It's not a big deal, Gabe," Charlie said. "We can wait a few more hours—"

"I'm done with waiting," Gabe said through clenched teeth. "I want to finish this mission."

"Fine!" Charlie shouted in his face. "You want this quest to be over with so fast, then that sounds great. Let's call her up."

Gabe didn't know why Charlie was suddenly so upset with him. He just wanted to get to the next ingredient, so they could become vampires faster. Isn't that what he wanted too?

Charlie swirled his fingers around until a small portal appeared by their heads. In the portal was Maria, who looked concerned.

"Are you boys, okay?" she asked.

Charlie rolled his eyes. "Yeah, except he," he said while pointing at Gabe, "wants to know what's taking so long."

Maria narrowed her eyes, making Gabe squirm and take a step back. He already had one witch mad at him; he didn't need two.

"Maybe it's because I'm having to do this in secret. Do you know what it's like to lie to your mother? Create a map for two idiots across the world? Did you ever think about how hard this has been for me?" she asked as she leaned closer and closer to the portal, shaking her closed fist.

"Sorry," Gabe whispered.

She sat back on her knees and patted the wrinkles out of her dress.

"It's fine. Though, it'll be a while until you receive your next map. My mother has been keeping an eye on me, and I've only been able to work in the middle of the night. You probably won't receive your next map until sundown," she explained.

Charlie looked at the pitch-black sky. "But it's way past sundown."

"Time zones, Charlie," Gabe reminded him again. "It's morning where she is."

"Right, and unless you want my mother to turn you both into fertilizer, I suggest you don't contact me again, unless there's an emergency, alright?" They nodded.

She leaned down, grabbed a small, tan bag, and handed it to them through the portal. "You're going to need to take the rest of the ingredients for a while. I fear if my mother finds them, she will grow suspicious of what we are doing." Charlie took the bag and put it in their sack. "I'll send the next map as soon as I can," she said then her picture disappeared.

"Well, I guess we should find somewhere to sleep," Charlie said, and Gabe agreed. He'd rather their mission take a little longer than have his parents receive a letter explaining his body was being used to grow pumpkins.

"Somewhere with a bed," Gabe suggested. The faster he fell asleep, the faster they would get their new map and the faster he'd be able to get home.

"Yeah, preferably," Charlie said as he cracked his back. "I feel like an old man."

"Well, remember this feeling, 'cause you'll never feel it again," Gabe said with a grin, expecting Charlie to give him one in return.

Instead, Charlie looked away. He bit the inside of his cheek and said, "Yeah."

"Are you okay?" Gabe asked. Charlie looked like he was about to say something when he changed his mind and forced a smile.

"Duh, we're about to become vampires," Charlie said as he gave Gabe his fakest smile. "Come on. Let's go."

Gabe followed Charlie down the path and to the street's sidewalk. They walked down the streets with nothing lighting their path except the flashlight, moon, and occasional car. Neither boy said a word, yet Gabe had many swirling in his mind.

Why was Charlie so upset? Gabe wondered. This had been his idea all along, so wouldn't he be glad Gabe was taking it so seriously? Wouldn't he be excited to be so close to the end?

They stopped in front of a small, grey, stone welcome center.

"They probably have brochures for places to sleep," Gabe suggested.

Charlie's eyes lit up. "Yeah, maybe they do." He placed Bearison's hood over his face then said, "Let's go."

Inside was almost empty, except for a man who was standing behind the counter, closing blinds. He turned to look at them then pointed to the clock on the wall.

"Oh," Gabe said, his cheeks flushed, "he must be closing up," he whispered to Charlie.

Charlie pushed Gabe towards the bathroom. "We'll be fast," he said to the man, "My friend has to go really bad."

Gabe had no idea why Charlie wanted him to go to the bathroom, but he figured he had a plan, and if he learned anything from the last twenty-four hours, it was that Charlie's plans somehow always had a way of working out.

As Gabe waited with his back pressed against the far wall of the restroom, he wondered what on earth Charlie could be planning now. Did he force him to go to the bathroom to buy them some time or was he expecting Gabe to cause a flood that distracted the man, so they could take his car keys and drive to some hotel? It wouldn't be the craziest thing they've done.

A few moments later, Charlie side-stepped into the bathroom with a mischievous grin on his face and his hands held behind his back.

"I got one," Charlie said as he held out his hand and waved a brochure in front of his face.

Gabe sighed, thankful his friend had gone with idea number one. He pushed himself off the wall and headed towards the exit, but when he tried to pass Charlie, the other boy held his arm out, stopping Gabe from going any farther.

"Oh, Gabe, still on silly human brain. Why walk all the way when we can use a little"— he waved his fingers around—"magic."

Gabe didn't know if he wanted to be pulled through another portal. He had a bruise on his hip from being thrown onto the mountain that morning. Or was it last night? The time zone thing had really messed with his mind. But another small bruise sounded better than walking miles and miles in the darkness of night.

"Sure, let's do it."

Charlie waved his hands around in a circle until another portal appeared. Gabe figured they'd step through together, but instead, he was pushed towards the portal before the picture could fully form.

His leg was yanked, and he was thrown onto the rough ground. This time his elbow took most of the damage.

"Ow," he said as he lifted his now bruised and scraped arm. That was a bad idea because apparently, he was on the side of a hill, and that arm had been supporting him. When he lifted it, his body leaned to the left, and he tumbled down the tough hill. He was thrown back and forth as the hill caved in until he landed on the cold, hard ground. His shoulders, back, and knees caught the brunt of the damage. He was sure he was bleeding and had multiple bruises, but at least his head didn't hit against the rocks.

Wait a minute. Why was he surrounded by rocks? And why was his foot wet?

"Ahh!" Charlie screamed as he, too, tumbled down the side of the mountain and landed right beside Gabe. Bearison had jumped out of Charlie's arms as soon as they had made it through the portal, so he gently guided himself down the side of the hill unscathed.

Gabe grabbed Charlie's flashlight and looked at his surroundings. They were not in a luscious hotel or any hotel for that matter. They weren't even inside. They were standing in between two mountains that edges met to form a river. He flashed the light around, trying to find any kind of place that could be considered a hotel, but there was nothing. They were alone with nature.

Gabe stormed over to Charlie. "Where are we?"

Charlie held his arms out. "Surprise. I was looking at the brochures, trying to find a place to stay, when I saw this one with an Onsen, which is like a hot tub, but it's heated by the nearby volcanic activity, and I was like, well, we have to go there before we leave, but you don't want to add any time to our trip, so I figured we could sleep here." He punched Gabe's shoulder. "Come on. It'll be like old times."

Gabe's head began to pulse as though his heart had moved from his chest to his skull. He didn't want to spend another night terrified of what could attack them. They'd already come across one life-threatening animal, and they'd been there less than two days.

"Oh, yeah, just like old times. Like when we would get bit by mosquitos or when you peed yourself because you were too scared to go inside and ask my parents to use the bathroom," Gabe said, "Why did you think that I would want to sleep outside again?"

Charlie frowned. He eyed Gabe up and down while shaking his head. "You know what? You're right. I don't think I know what you want anymore."

Charlie grabbed the sack from Gabe's shoulder and headed towards the edge of the mountain. He placed the sack down and laid his head on it, facing away from Gabe.

Great, now he was upset again, Gabe thought. What did Charlie even have to be upset about? He had everything he wanted. Sure, his parents weren't perfect, but he'd never been woken up in the middle of the night by his mom screaming at his dad because she thought something was staring at them from outside the window. He'd never been picked up early from school by his father who took him to get ice cream, only to then explain he had to take his mother to a mental hospital for treatment again. He didn't have to drag a ladder across the kitchen, so he could reach the microwave when he was in kindergarten because his mother wasn't well enough to make him lunch.

He didn't have to give up the rest of his childhood to become a vampire to keep his family safe.

To Charlie, becoming a vampire meant fun adventures and crime-fighting and visiting volcanoes. To Gabe, it meant growing up and becoming a man, a protector.

He lay beside Charlie, his head on the other edge of the sack, and closed his eyes. Tomorrow, he would get the last ingredient, and Maria would turn him into a vampire. Tomorrow, he would be strong enough to protect his mother. Tomorrow he was going to have everything he wanted.

He took a few deep breaths and tried to calm himself enough to sleep, ignoring the doubt that still sat in the back of his mind.

Chapter 15: The Collision

Gabe was woken by something licking his face.

"Ugh, Bearison," he whined as he pushed the bear away, so he could sit up. He regretted doing so. His bruises had turned blue and purple, and they were way bigger than he originally thought. His shoulder was covered in scrapes that burned every time he moved his arm, and his back made a crinkling sound as though he were tap-dancing on bubble wrap.

It wasn't until he was sitting up that he noticed Charlie had moved from beside him. He was sitting by the small Onsen, which was surrounded by a small mountain of rocks. Charlie had his pants rolled up and was dangling his feet in the steaming water. He seemed concentrated on the water, as though he were in deep thought about the mechanics of how a volcano nearby heated this tiny pool of water, off the side of the river that rushed by.

Gabe checked the map. 'Await further instructions' was still written on the off-white, unrolled paper. He slipped the map back into the sack and made his way over to Charlie. He had to know why his friend was so upset with him. So, he didn't want to sleep under the stars? So, he didn't want to stop and look at a waterfall? Did those things matter that much to Charlie?

He sat beside Charlie, took off his, now dry, high-tops, and dipped his feet in the Onsen. The warmth crept from his toes to his stomach, as if he were drinking a warm mug of hot cocoa. He closed his eyes and bathed in the feeling while trying to think of ways to ask Charlie what was wrong without belittling his problems.

His mother had always told him that though someone else's problem might seem small to him, it might be big to them, and it didn't do anyone any good to make someone feel worse than they already were. Telling someone their problem was stupid or laughable didn't make the other person less angry; it only made them feel bad for feeling bad. It'd be better to say nothing at all.

But Gabe didn't want this hanging over their heads for the rest of the mission. He wanted Charlie to tell him all the things that were bugging him, and then they could get going on their trip.

"Does that hurt?" Gabe asked as he pointed to Charlie's scraped knee. Charlie shook his head.

"No, I've been attacked by so many wild animals, this was nothing."

Gabe rolled his eyes. Same old Charlie.

Charlie pointed to Gabe's bruised shoulder and winced. "I bet that hurts pretty bad."

Gabe peaked at his shoulder. His dark blue shoulder. It felt like someone had thrown a brick at him. "Nope, can't even feel it."

Charlie grinned. "Well, then, guess you won't care if I do this then." Before Gabe could ask what, Charlie pushed him into the water.

It was warm, but it was still filled with who knows what kind of algae and little creatures. It only went down a couple feet, so Gabe got to his knees and pushed his head out of the water, shaking out his hair.

"What was that for?" Gabe shouted, making Charlie laugh. He raised his shoulders.

"Because it was funny." He laughed so hard he grabbed his stomach and bent over. "You should see your face."

Gabe frowned. He didn't need to see his face. He was the one making it, and he was angry. His arms tensed as he moved his knees closer and closer to Charlie.

Charlie tried to stand and run away, but before he could even get to his feet, Gabe grabbed his leg and pulled him into the water. When Charlie jumped up and started spitting the dirty water out of his mouth, Gabe began to feel a little better.

"Now you should see the look on your face," Gabe said with a laugh. Charlie was trying to squirt all the water from his nose, and it was gross. Once his nasal passage was clean, he wiped his eyes and smiled.

"Oh, it's on," he said as he lunged at Gabe. They were both careful since the Onsen was shallow and surrounded by rocks, but they still got a few kicks and punches in. Being under the water and messing around with his best friend brought Gabe a sense of relief he hadn't had in months. The only thing he had to worry about at this moment was dodging Charlie's attempt to put his foot on his face.

After a few too many kicks to his bad shoulder, Gabe jumped out of the water and yelled, "Truce!"

Charlie nodded, out of breath. They moved to the side and rested their heads along the rocks to calm down.

"That was fun," Gabe said as he looked off between the mountains to where the river took a sharp turn.

"Yeah," Charlie said while staring at the sun, something he did because his mother always told him not to. "Hey, Gabe?"

Gabe turned his head to look at Charlie. "Yeah?"

"Why don't we wait?"

"Wait for what?" Gabe asked.

Charlie looked away from the sun, blinked a few times, then turned to watch his fingers tap against his knee. "Wait to become vampires."

Gabe stood. "What are you talking about? Why would we wait?" He wasn't seriously having doubts now, right when they were about to be done.

Charlie stood and pulled at the edge of his t-shirt, wringing it out. "I just realized we, maybe, hadn't really thought things through yet. I mean, this is a big deal."

Of course, it's a big deal, Gabe thought. "What's changed? This was your idea?"

Charlie shrugged. "I don't know. After we talked to that guy at the restaurant, it got me thinking. I'm not sure I'm ready to become a vampire. Maybe we should wait until we're eighteen. Then we can travel and have fun without having to worry about people seeing us as kids."

Gabe's shoulders tensed. He climbed out of the Onsen and clenched his fists. How could Charlie do this to him?

"I can't wait, Charlie. We have to do this now," Gabe said as he removed his shirt and replaced it with one of the ones Charlie had bought the day before.

Charlie climbed out of the Onsen and made his way over to Gabe. "I just think that we should get the last ingredient and hold on to them until we're older. I don't want to regret this decision."

"I can't believe this," Gabe said as he kicked the mountain's side. "I can't believe you would change your mind after everything we've gone through. You came to me with this idea. You wanted me to know all about witches and vampires and everything, then you begged me to go with you on this trip, and now, you don't even want to become vampires." Gabe turned around and shook his fist. "Do you realize how important this is to me?"

"No!" Charlie screamed back in Gabe's face. His eyes shined, and Gabe knew it wasn't from the Onsen. "No, because you haven't talked to me the whole time we've been on our quest. You are so focused on going home. I thought this would be a fun journey for us to go on together, but you've sucked all the fun out of it."

Gabe waved his arms in the air. "Well, I'm sorry this has been hard for you, but it hasn't exactly been easy for me either."

"Then tell me what's wrong," Charlie said, his voice breaking, "because this whole time you've been acting weird. Don't think I didn't see you crying in the mall. I thought you missed your parents or something, so I didn't say anything, but now I'm thinking you don't want to be my friend anymore."

How could Charlie think that? He was Gabe's best friend. They'd done everything together. Gabe wanted so badly to tell him everything about the past few months. About how his mom had been getting worse and worse and how his Papa worked so much he barely saw him, but that's not what grown men did. They don't cry to their friends about their problems; they keep them inside and deal with them alone.

"Well, sorry I'm not good company, but some of us have real problems to deal with!" Gabe shouted. "Some of us have to grow up. Some things are more important than our friendship. Some of us have families that actually care about each other."

He knew he'd taken it too far as soon as he saw the betrayal cross Charlie's face. He couldn't believe he'd yelled that at his best friend. He just wanted him to understand what he was going through. He didn't want to hurt him.

Charlie stared at the ground beside Gabe's feet, something he always did to stop himself from crying. He bit his lip and nodded to the side. "I'm going to check on Bearison."

"Charlie, I—" Gabe started but then stopped himself. He couldn't think of anything to say. There was no way an 'I'm sorry' was going to make up for telling his best friend his parents didn't care for him.

Why was everything and everyone out to get him? He wanted to go back to the way things used to be. When he could have fun and focus on homework and video games and trying to hit the ball at baseball practice. He wanted to be carefree again.

He wanted to be a kid again.

It wasn't fair. It wasn't fair that he had to grow up faster than his friends. It wasn't fair he had to learn how to calm himself down, so he didn't get angry at his parents when they were late picking him up from school or when he woke up on Saturdays to a new babysitter because his dad was out looking for his mom again. When was it going to be his turn to have a break?

Gabe's head started pulsing, his vision became dark, and he wanted so badly to scream, to let all the anger and sadness and fear out of his head. He wanted to let it out. Just as he was about to punch the mountain's side, Charlie ran back to him with wide, terrified eyes.

"Gabe," Charlie said, with his hands on his knees as he tried to catch his breath. "Bearison, he's missing."

Chapter 16: The Release

They grabbed their sack and ran down beside the river in the direction they'd last seen Bearison.

"Bearison!" Charlie screamed, turning in circles to make sure the bear wasn't behind them. "Come on, Bearison! Where are you?" His voice shook as he ran farther and farther from the Onsen. Gabe tried to keep up but losing his "pet" caused Charlie to go into protective mom mode and develop incredible speed.

After a while, Charlie stopped and turned to climb up the side of the mountain. Every time Gabe moved his shoulder to grab for a ledge or rock, the pain would shoot down his arm, but he had to help Charlie find the bear. Maybe if they found him, he'd be so happy he'd forgive Gabe.

Eventually, they reached the top of the mountain, which was a wide, dimly lit forest.

"Bearison?" Charlie asked quieter, as though he thought something was lurking in the forest with them and hoped it had bad hearing. "Come on buddy."

"Maybe he found a mama?" Gabe asked.

Charlie flashed his flashlight in Gabe's face. "You think he found a mama bear and what? We didn't notice a giant brown bear walk past us to take him away?"

Gabe shrugged. "Weirder things have happened." He didn't have much hope in his words, but the woods seemed to go on forever, and they hadn't seen any sign of Bearison. No tracks, growls, nothing bumping into their legs. Nothing to show he was still nearby.

Charlie turned and continued walking. "Well, your opinion doesn't matter anyway 'cause I'm not talking to you."

Gabe wanted to apologize for saying his parents didn't care about him and making him doubt their friendship. Instead, he let his anger take over and said, "Fine, well I'm not talking to you either."

They continued through the woods in silence. The farther they got from the river, the more Gabe felt the need to pee. But if he stopped, Charlie would probably go on without him, and if he asked him to stop, that would mean Charlie had won in the, who could stay quiet the longest challenge.

Luckily, he didn't have to do either because Charlie broke his vow of silence when he said, "I can't believe you said some things are more important than our friendship. Nothing is more important than our friendship. If I had a huge gymnastics competition one weekend and on the same weekend you needed one of my lungs or something, I'd donate it to you in a second."

Gabe wanted so badly to hold back his laughter. He didn't want to make Charlie feel like an idiot, but the pressure was building in the back of his throat, climbing up like a ladder, until it burst out his mouth as a chuckle. He hit his knees and threw his head back, laughing harder than he ever had.

Charlie narrowed his eyes so much, Gabe wasn't even sure they were open. "What?" he spat. "I'm being serious."

Gabe tried to catch his breath and explain what was so funny, but the stress had been building in him every day since his Mama's medicine stopped working, and he couldn't hold it back any longer. Maybe he wasn't allowed to cry, but he could laugh.

Gabe nodded furiously. "I know, I know I—," he let out a snort. "You can't donate a lung when your still alive, Charlie. They're not like kidneys. You need both to survive."

Charlie scowled. "That is so not the point."

Gabe continued to nod. "I know, I just..." He sighed. "I needed that."

Charlie hit his knees beside him and bowed his head. "We're not gonna find him, are we?"

Gabe stopped laughing and frowned, shaking his head. "I don't think so."

They lay back in the dirt, side by side. Gabe could hear his mother shouting at him to not get his baseball pants dirty, but it had been over twenty-four hours since he'd put them on, and they already needed a good wash.

He looked over at Charlie, who was frowning at the sky. Gabe wished he didn't understand why Charlie was hesitating about their decision. He wished he could be mad at Charlie for changing his mind, but how could he after wanting to change his own mind multiple times? The only thing Charlie did was be honest, something Gabe didn't have the courage to do.

Or maybe he did. Maybe he could tell Charlie all he was going through. He'd never been rude, laughed, or made Gabe feel lesser than. He never told Gabe to keep his chin up and be a man. He let him be himself.

"My mom got hurt, and I couldn't save her," Gabe said. "That's why I came with you because I thought if I became a vampire, I would be strong enough to help protect her. That's what's more important than our friendship."

Charlie sat up and leaned against his elbows. "Why didn't you just tell me that? I would've understood."

Gabe shrugged against the ground. "Because, my family, they like to hide when my mom is doing bad. They think people will look at us differently. Either like they feel sorry for us or like they're better than us. Both suck."

"Well, you know I'd never look at you any different, so be honest with me next time, okay?"

Gabe leaned up. "Do you really not want to become vampires anymore?"

Charlie wrapped his arms around his knees. "I don't know. I don't think so. I just, I thought if we got turned it meant I wouldn't have to get older. My parents have always said getting older is the worst thing ever. You have bigger problems to deal with, and you gotta earn a bunch of money just to like, live, and all they ever do is fight. I thought if I turned into a vampire, I'd never turn into them."

Gabe sat up and crossed his legs. He rubbed his fingers across the place between his eyes as tears threatened to spill. "I don't want to be a vampire, either. I don't know what else to do. My dad's not home to watch my mom all the time, and I gotta be the man, but I'm not a man, you know? So, how am I supposed to protect my mom like one?"

Charlie threw his arm around Gabe's shoulder. He didn't say anything; there wasn't anything to say. He didn't have any answers.

"I'm sorry, man. I wish I had never brought any of this up. The vampires, the dumb witches!" Charlie shoved Gabe's knee. "Wait a minute. The witches. Why didn't we think of this before?"

Gabe grabbed his friends' shoulders and asked, "What are you going on about?"

"Maybe the witches can help your mom."

Gabe's eyes widened. "Oh, my gosh, you're right. Why didn't I think of that? These people can turn humans into monsters and heal wounds with vegetables and herbs; maybe they can heal my mom?"

Charlie shrugged. "It's worth a shot."

"Wow, we're really not that smart," Gabe said while grinning.

"We are not." Charlie chuckled. "I thought you could donate a lung."

They sighed delighted sighs.

"So," Charlie said, "does this mean we're going home?"

Gabe looked at the sack as it began to glow. He unzipped it and pulled out the map which now had a line sketched across it. The X was not too far from the dot that represented where they currently stood. They could make it there within the hour.

Gabe threw the sack over his shoulder and said, "We're already so close. Who knows, maybe we'll change our minds one day. Then we won't have to scour an island again. What do you say? One last quest?"

Charlie threw his arm around Gabe. "One last quest."

Chapter 17: The Last Ingredient

The map led deeper into the forest.

They relied more and more on the light of the flashlight, even as the sun rose higher into the sky. The trees grew closer together, so Gabe had to stand behind Charlie to get through. Their path was short, but their trip was lengthened by them stopping every few seconds to check out a sound from behind them.

Gabe had his back turned as he kept moving, so he didn't notice Charlie stop until he bumped into his back.

"Ahh!" he screamed until he realized who it was.

"Shh," Charlie said, with his finger over his lips. "There's something out here," he whispered. "I can feel it."

All Gabe could feel was a cold breeze and the urgent turn of his stomach. He should've listened to it earlier in the trip. Then he wouldn't be standing next to his one-trick pony of a friend, with only a flashlight and a leather sack, heading deeper and deeper into the dangerous woods.

"Why did you stop?" Gabe asked.

Charlie pointed his flashlight ahead. Standing ten feet in front of them was a ginormous cave. It had vines growing over it, starting on one side and ending on the other. The inside of the cave was dark, and the boys had no idea what lurked inside. The front of the cave was narrow, but the farther back it went, the longer it grew until the boys couldn't see either end.

"This is where the map ends," Charlie said. He ran his flashlight along the edges of the cave, and that's when they noticed the six feet tall, stone statues that lined the outside. They were men wearing armor, and they had swords in their hands, pointed down at their feet. "Awesome," Charlie said as he headed over to touch one.

Gabe grabbed his arm. "Not awesome. If there are statues here, then someone probably lives around here. Someone creepy and possibly dangerous."

Charlie took a step back. "Yeah, that makes sense. Let's find the Coninm Mactumla—"

"Conium Maculatum," Gabe corrected.

"Right, Conium Maculatum, and get out of here."

"Oh, I don't think you boys are going anywhere," someone whispered from the cave. The voice was sharp, scratchy, as though it were a song playing on a record, and someone was moving the needle back and forth, preventing it from catching the tune.

They turned and froze when they noticed the woman exit the cave. She had a long, flowing purple dress, was barefoot, and had her palms raised defensively, purple lights glowing from her hands.

"Oh, um, hello," Gabe said. "My friend and I mean no harm. We were wondering if you wouldn't mind sparing a little bit of your, um, herbs from your garden? We understand if that's a problem, uh, ma'am."

The woman let out a humorless chuckle before the lights around her hand grew darker. "Oh, you boys think you're so adorable. You think I'm some helpless lady who wants to give away my hard work to you because you're young and have sweet faces. But you are trespassing on my property, and I want to know why?"

Just as Gabe was about to make up some explanation about a stupid prank, Charlie's knees hit the ground and he squeezed the sides of his head with his hands.

"Ow!" he screamed as he shook his head back and forth. He threw his forehead on the ground and pushed it forward, as though it was too heavy to hold up.

Gabe leaned down and placed his hand on Charlie's back. "Charlie, what's wrong?"

Charlie groaned and hit his fist against the ground. Judging by how he squeezed his eyes shut, he seemed to be in a lot of pain.

Gabe stormed up to the witch and screamed, "Stop, you're hurting him!"

The witch was not staring at Charlie, but instead at her hands, which had stopped glowing. Her jaw dropped as she looked at Charlie, who seemed to be in worse shape as his whole body shook.

"This is impossible," the woman said, taking a step back. "You shouldn't be alive. You should be dead. You were all dead."

"What are you talking about?" Gabe shouted. "He didn't do anything wrong, so stop this now!"

"I'm not doing anything to your friend," the woman said, as though she didn't believe what she was saying. "Your friend is doing this to himself."

"Why would my friend be putting himself in pain?" Gabe asked. He wanted to go back to Charlie, but before he could get over to him, the witch raised her hands and the vines around the cave rose. They grabbed Gabe's arms and held him back.

"No!" he screamed. Why was this woman hurting Charlie? He thought. Why wouldn't she let them leave?

The woman pointed at Charlie, and the vines wrapped around him and carried him into the cave. The woman walked in after him, and Gabe was dragged in behind them as he kicked his feet against the sandy bottom.

She had the vines drop Charlie onto a wooden chair and wrap his legs to the chair's legs, his arms tied behind his back. Gabe was placed beside him in another chair, his arms and legs tied similarly.

Charlie's face was bright red. He bit so hard on his lip, it drew a small amount of blood. With every second, he became closer and closer to passing out.

"Now, tell me everything about what you are doing here and who sent you," the woman said, her thin, wrinkled lips pushed out as though she had drunk something vile.

Charlie couldn't speak, so Gabe spoke for him. "No one sent us. We were at the nearby Onsen, and we decided to see how close we could get to the cave without getting attacked by an animal."

Wow, Gabe couldn't believe he came up with that on the spot. Maybe after spending all this time with Charlie some of his skills were rubbing off on him.

The woman clenched her fist, and the vines became tighter, digging into his wrists and ankles.

"Now, do you want to try that again? This time, with the truth." She clenched her fist, and the vines grew even tighter, so tight, he couldn't feel his hands.

Then the vines fell away, onto the floor. Gabe squeezed his fingers and toes as blood rushed back to them. He didn't take a moment to think about why they'd become free. He reached for Charlie, whose vines had also fallen away, and picked him up.

"Where do you think you're going?" the woman screamed, reaching her arms out to the boys, but nothing happened, as though the vines had chosen not to listen to her anymore. She stared at her hands in horror.

Gabe took the time she was distracted to get out of the cave. Once they reached the exit, Charlie was able to stand on his own, and the terrible pain had reduced to a small ache.

They ran along the side of the cave, not taking the time to look back until they had put a long distance between them and the witch.

"Quick, portal us home," Gabe said. Charlie nodded and created a portal for Maria. A wide circle of flowing fields appeared. Gabe went to take a step, but he couldn't get through. It was as if a force field had placed itself in the portal.

Charlie tried to put his own foot through, but he too couldn't get past the force field either.

"Maria!" Charlie shouted, hoping she was close by. She appeared with wide eyes.

"What's wrong?" she asked, running to stand behind one of the huts.

"Why can't we get through the portal?" Charlie asked as he looked back to the cave's entrance.

"Have you gotten the last ingredient?" she asked.

"Uh, no," Charlie said. "We got attacked by an old, witch lady. Thanks for the warning by the way."

Maria frowned. She looked between them and said, "You're still there. No wonder you can't portal back. You need to get far away from her place. She might have a magic dampener surrounding her property. Grab the last ingredient and get back."

"No time," Charlie said. "We've changed our minds. We're going to go home." He looked around and pointed to a straight line between the trees. "Let's go that way."

"Charlie?" Gabe whispered with a groggy voice.

Charlie turned to Gabe who was standing frozen by the cave, staring down at the stone sword sticking through his chest.

Chapter 18: The Resurrection

Neither boy knew what to do.

They stood and watched as the stone soldier pulled the sword out of Gabe's back and stood back in its position.

"Gabe?" Charlie asked as he watched his friend hit his knees.

"Charlie?" Gabe asked, half awake. His eyes rolled in the back of his head, and he slipped to the ground.

"Gabe!" Charlie screamed. He ran and kneeled beside his best friend. He gathered him into his arms and shook him, trying to wake him up. "Come on, Gabe. You're going to be okay. You gotta wake up." A tear dropped onto Gabe's hair as Charlie screamed, "Wake up, Gabe!"

He didn't move. He felt like he weighed a ton, making Charlie's arms shake beneath him.

"Come on!" he shouted. "I lied; the Nintendo was for you. Now wake up and yell at me for lying."

"Get him away and keep moving," Maria said as she checked behind him. "Hopefully, you can get him back in time and we can help him."

Charlie nodded and lifted his friend as he stood. Gabe was heavy, but the adrenaline rushing through Charlie's arms was more than enough as he ran through the woods. Every so often, he would push his elbow against the portal as it floated beside him, but there was still a force field.

Eventually, Gabe's weight became too much, and Charlie hit his knees.

"I can't keep going. This forest could go on for miles. I can't-I can't save him."

He placed his fingers on his friend's neck to check his pulse, which had grown weak. "He's not gonna make it."

Charlie couldn't believe what was happening. He had to be dreaming. His best friend wasn't going to die. He wasn't going to die on their stupid quest. Charlie pinched himself and screamed when he felt the pain rush through his arm. He didn't scream for the physical pain though, for the emotional pain cut through him like a knife.

"I'm sorry!" he sobbed as he held the sides of his best friend's face. "This is all my fault. I never should've"—Charlie wiped his nose—"never should've asked you to join me on this stupid quest. This was never going to work out. I never even wanted to be a vampire. I just wanted to have a fun quest with you."

Wait a minute, Charlie thought as he rubbed his red eyes. He might die, but that doesn't mean he has to stay dead. "I'll be right back," he told Gabe.

Charlie jumped to his feet and ran back to the cave. He didn't care if he was putting himself in danger; he had to save Gabe, no matter what the cost.

He got to the vines and pulled a handful of leaves off, shoving them in his pocket.

"Where do you think you're going?" the witch asked as she reached her arms out and controlled the vines to grab Charlie's wrists. "You may be a Detros, but you are untrained, and I will not let you get away again."

Charlie gave all his strength to pull at the vines, but he was tired. He fell to his knees.

Then something crept up behind the witch. Something eight feet tall, with brown fur and sharp teeth. It got down to all fours and let out a roar so low, the ground shook. The witch turned and stared at the bear. She looked down at her hands controlling the vines, as though trying to decide whether Charlie or the bear was a bigger threat.

The bear took slow, threatening steps towards the witch, snarling its teeth. That's when Charlie noticed a particular feature on this big, brown bear's face. It's upturned nose.

No, it couldn't be, Charlie thought. Bearison's mother was gone.

But then a baby bear came out from behind the mama and ran over to Charlie, nuzzling his nose against Charlie's leg.

"Bearison?" Charlie asked. Bearison plopped his butt on the ground and bopped his nose against Charlie's leg again as if saying yes.

The witch turned and squeezed her hand, making the vines tighten and Charlie scream.

Bearison didn't seem to like watching his friend scream. He took a few steps back before turning to the witch and charging at her. He jumped and opened his mouth, biting her arm.

She shouted in pain and dropped her hands, making the vines fall off Charlie's arms. He darted through the forest, running until he heard a tiny roar behind him. He turned and saw the witch had thrown Bearison, and the baby bear was now lying on its stomach. A piece of his brown fur right above his eye had turned purple from the blast.

Mama Bearison didn't like watching her baby get blasted, so she went after the witch. Charlie didn't have any time to waste; he had to get back to Gabe, but he kept his eyes on Bearison for a moment longer. Just long enough to see the bear look up at him and bow his head, as though to say, good luck my friend.

Charlie ran through the woods until he found Gabe. The portal was still open beside him, Maria watching over Gabe with narrow eyes.

"Okay," Charlie said as he hit his knees and unzipped the bag. "I have the last ingredient. How do I change him into a vampire?"

Maria, who was now sitting in her hut, grabbed her book and read through it. "First thing you need to do is combine all the ingredients in the small stone bowl I put in the bag." Charlie grabbed the bowl and put all the herbs together. "You'll need to smash them with the pestle." Charlie raised his brow, making Maria roll her eyes. "The weird hammer. Smash them with the weird hammer."

Charlie grabbed the short, thick baseball-shaped object from the bag and smashed the herbs into little bits.

"What now?" he asked.

"Now you need to put a little bit of your, um, own blood into the bowl."

Charlie had no limit of scrapes and cuts. His most recent was a scraped knee from when the witch attacked him. He wiped a little of the blood into the bowl.

"Add the water," Maria said. Charlie grabbed the glass water bottle and poured it over the herbs in the bowl. "And say these words."

She said a few words in Latin, which Charlie repeated. The mixture turned into one, combined brown liquid. "Pour it down his throat."

He picked up Gabe's head and poured the mixture down his throat.

"Now what?" Charlie asked.

"Now you have to offer him to the earth. If it deems him worthy, he will be returned to you," she explained.

"What if the earth decides it's his time to go?" Charlie asked.

Maria frowned and looked away. Obviously, it didn't mean anything good. He figured it didn't matter. He had to try.

"How do I offer him to the earth?" Charlie asked.

"You're going to have to dig him a grave."

Charlie didn't have any sort of digging tools, but he wasn't going to give up. He scratched and dug at the ground for hours until there was a hole deep enough for Gabe. He lowered Gabe into the hole, covered him with the dirt, and sat beside him.

"What now?" he asked.

"Now you wait."

He waited for what felt like days. The sun rose to the tip of the sky and fell behind him. Charlie didn't move; it felt like he didn't even breathe. He stared at the grave he'd dug for his best friend and waited. Maria had to go after a few hours since it was almost daylight for her, but she made him promise to contact her as soon as Gabe made any changes.

He waited and waited and waited. With every hour that passed, he grew a little more afraid the earth wasn't going to give him his best friend back. He grew afraid of being alone. He grew afraid of never being able to forgive himself after being the one to convince his friend to come along on this stupid journey in the first place.

He clasped his hands together and pleaded to whatever or whoever was listening. "Please, bring him back. Please. His parents need him. I need him." He placed his hands on the grave, his arms shaking. "Please."

His flashlight, which had been propped up on his sack offering a ray of light in the dark forest, flickered before shutting off.

"Oh, come on!" he shouted as he picked up the flashlight and hit it a few times before throwing it on the ground. How much longer was this going to take?

The ground shook beside him. He was in pitch blackness, so dark he couldn't even see his own hand, but he could feel the change in the dirt. He could hear it shifting beside him, before a pair of bright red eyes stared at him, as though looking right into his soul.

The eyes of his best friend.

Gabe and Charlie will return...

Made in the USA
Middletown, DE
27 October 2023